SNOWED INN (WITH A DEMON)

L.E. ELDRIDGE

Book Cover by Clover Lane Designs

Illustrations by Eleanora Panepinto

Beta Read by Chloe Parker and Anne Riland

To Jackie Wildermouth. Who may not have liked this book, but is the reason I wrote it.

CONTENTS

CONTENT WARNING

Though this story isn't dark, I wanted to add a content warning for anyone who may want some warning about the kind of sex scenes in this book.

This book contains explicit sex scenes and is meant for audiences 18 and older. This book contains, primal play, tail play, impact play, and light BDSM.

Enjoy :)

1

TANA

R oll, Roll, Clink.

The perfume was on the floor...again.

Tana sighed and turned around to pick up the plastic bottle. Her cat, Binx, had been sitting on her lap the whole time, so it wasn't her. And she was sure she put it on the flat end but it rolled off anyway. *Probably that damn ghost*, she thought, but immediately pushed that thought aside. There's no such thing as ghosts and Tana knew that. And even if there was, it seemed like acknowledging it would only make things worse.

The Camden Inn she lived and worked in drew a lot of their clients from the lore of the ghost, and it was all bullshit. According to all these crazed ghost sites, there was a huge accident here back in the 1800s; a huge fire that killed everyone inside.

Even though the house was built in 1810, there'd never been a fire here and there sure had never been any deaths. Tana had done a lot of research before deciding to work here. She didn't believe in ghosts per se, but if people were dying left and right, she wasn't taking that risk.

It was just a sprawling Georgian-style mansion-turned-inn with a creaky old gate and surrounded by forest. The owner, Mrs. Camden, liked the older style, so there was a lot of vintage mismatched furniture and elaborate wallpaper. Plus, these stories brought in a ton of business, meaning Tana had to nod and hold back her eye rolls whenever guests talked about it or when she was hosting a tour.

There were some weird things that happened here and tons of visitors claimed it happened to them. Some even left in the middle of the night. Though these cases were few and far between, they caused quite a stir among the remaining guests, leaving everyone curious about what happened.

For Tana, the worst that had happened was her perfume bottle falling and shattering. Her room smelled like roses and cedar for months after. She'd then switched to plastic.

"Tan," she heard with a knock on the other side of the door.

Damn.

Tana finished her last flick of mascara and then capped the tube. She got up and opened the door. Kaya stood on the other side, worrying the hem of her sweater. Her blonde, straight hair was half up, her big, green doe eyes filled with nerves.

She was a nineteen-year-old college freshman, and surprisingly, the inn's hardest worker. Most of the time, Tana didn't hire college students. Not that there was anything wrong with them, they just tended to be flaky. Not Kaya. She was a hotel management major and always took this job seriously, but she always got stressed when she had something to report.

"Sorry to bother you," she started, "I know your shift ended an hour ago and you were going to go out, so again I'm really sorry…"

"Kay," Tana said, cutting her off. "It's fine, what's going on."

"Yes, well, there's a man downstairs. His name is Cornelious Cander and apparently, he's some big ghost hunter online. I think I've watched him before, maybe. But anyway, he's downstairs. He requested a tour of the property even though I told him there aren't any scheduled till this weekend and he would have needed to schedule a private tour in advance. He turned all Karen on me and is now demanding he speak to the manager. Tyler is busy helping in the barn so..." she trailed off, staring at her with those big eyes.

Tana rubbed her temples, trying to stay calm. Tyler was her assistant manager, but with the snow coming, he'd been working on the generator to make sure the power didn't go out. And it wasn't Kaya's fault this guy was being a prick. It also wasn't her fault Tana lived at the inn instead of getting her own place. If she was honest with herself, she didn't have to live here. But she dreamed of one day owning an inn of her own, and to do that, she needed to save. And what a better way to save than free rent?

Tana pushed her curly hair up into a bun and grabbed her keys. She had plans tonight, but it wasn't anything that couldn't wait. Tana's friend Bea invited her out, and after ditching her one too many times, she wouldn't take no for an answer. They'd been friends since Tana moved here, but since becoming the general manager, she hadn't been able to see her as often. Tana would have to text her and let her know she would be a bit late.

She followed Kaya down the hall toward the lobby. When Tana got there, she was greeted by the familiar floral print walls, crackling fireplace, and mismatched antique furniture littering the space. The dark wood desk was to the left of the entrance, facing the stairs.

At said desk stood the man she assumed was Cornelious along with three other men holding a ton of equipment. Cornelious was average height, with brown hair and a jaw so tight it looked like he would break a tooth. He was traditionally attractive, but nothing special. His crew looked like photocopies, all with different shades of brown hair and average build.

Tana couldn't help but think they looked like the B-Movie version of Ghostbusters.

Tana walked up to Cornelious, throwing on her best customer service smile. "Hello, sir," she said, reaching her hand out to shake his. "My name is Tana. I'm the general manager here."

He eyed Tana up and down and she had to resist rolling her eyes. Even in this day and age, people still looked down on her as a woman in management. "Cornelius Cander, but you can call me Neil," He said, meeting her hand in greeting.

"Neil, excellent, how can I help you?"

"I have a reservation here for the next two nights. I wanted to do a private tour of some of the side buildings and maybe the basement or something. Somewhere you don't show on the normal tours. Oh! I even heard there's a haunted barn in the back where someone hung themselves or something. Your employee Katie here told me that wasn't possible, but I'm sure we can work something out."

Tana widened her smile, trying to hide her grimace. "Yes, well, unfortunately, we don't allow guests in closed-off areas without a guide and we have limited staff because of the storm coming, so we've canceled all our normal tours. We normally ask guests to schedule private tours ahead of time." She knew she sounded condescending, but with guests like this, it was better to make things as clear as possible.

"I appreciate that for *normal* guests, but I'm sure you know I make one of the largest ghost-hunting shows on the internet with thousands of viewers. Our show will bring you guys so much business. All things considered, I was going to request a free room."

His sleazy smile made Tana cringe internally. She knew his type; they came here a lot. Content creators who thought their clout would make them bend the rules for them, but Tana didn't do that.

"Sorry sir, we can't. It's against policy. But you're welcome to any of the places open to guests."

"Listen, Tammy, I'm sure you're just following the rules, but I'm sure we can come to some...other agreement." He waggled his brows suggestively.

Tana ignored the fact he called her the wrong name and focused on the task at hand. "Sorry, that's not possible. Would you like me to check you in?" she asked instead. Tana saw Kaya looking between the two of them, obviously uncomfortable with the conflict.

He quickly dropped the smirk, switching tactics. "Is there someone more...qualified I can talk to? A higher up perhaps?"

"Unfortunately not," she said in a clipped tone. "I am the highest-up manager in this state, and the owner is in Florida. Like I said earlier if you would have called before, we could have made the proper arrangements, but you didn't. So. You can either check-in and stick to the guest areas, or you can leave." She held her winning smile, but her words obviously angered him.

He started stepping closer, causing Tana to back up. "Listen, you obviously don't know–," he started, but before he could finish, he tripped and landed on his face. It was like the rug got pulled right out from under him. Tana could hear Kaya trying to cover her snicker with a cough and she had to school her own features.

She reached out to help him, but he shook her off, obviously embarrassed. "We'll just check in," he mumbled once he was upright again.

"Perfect, Kaya will finish checking y'all in." Kaya sprang into action, rounding the desk to check them in. Tana turned and headed back to her room with a genuine smile on her face.

On her way to the room, Tana's phone vibrated in her pocket. When she looked, Mom flashed across the screen. She debated ignoring it but decided it was better if she didn't. The wrath only ever increased the longer she stalled. She answered the call, lifting the phone to her ear with a deep sigh.

"Hi Mom," Tana said.

"Hi hon," her mom replied. "How are things?"

"Things are fine. Work's good, classes are over. Everything's going well."

"That's great. I'm so glad you're going back to school. Even if it is one of those online ones." Her mother held the opinion that online college was just fake college. She believed a brick-and-mortar education was the only way to learn, which definitely wasn't true. Tana excelled in her online education, unlike she had when she tried to go in person. "Anyway," her mom continued, "I just want to make sure everything is set for you to come home."

"Yes. I'm leaving Sunday morning. I'm hoping to beat the storm."

"Well, make sure you come. You know how important

the holidays are. Your aunt Melinda will be here, and I'm sure she'll bring your cousins. Oh, and we got an even bigger tree this year! Wait till you see it!"

Oh yes, Tana knew how important the holidays were. But in her house, they weren't important because of spending time with family like it was for others. In her house, it was a dick-measuring contest. Or in her mother's case, a bank account measuring contest. Her father was a lawyer and her mother managed a hedge fund before Tana was born. The holidays were the best time to show the rest of her almost equally successful family that they would always just be *almost.*

The fact that Tana worked at an inn instead of a law firm or hospital had always been a disappointment, and since she was an only child, it was an even bigger deal. But she liked her job and her life. "Yes, mom I'll be there."

They said their goodbyes and Tana sat back at her vanity, looking around her room. It was nothing fancy. Just another room that Mrs. Camden let her stay in. There was a fireplace to the side and her bed sat in the corner. There was a small attached bathroom with a bath and a dresser on the other side of the room, covered with jewelry and craft books. Even though it was just another room, Tana tried to make it her own.

At her parents, she wasn't allowed to decorate, even as a kid. Everything had to look clean and polished. Now she wasn't there, she took the opportunity to decorate. The walls were covered in macrame wall hangings and embroidery she'd made. She decided that if she really wanted to make her room *hers*; she wanted to make it herself.

Hobbies were another thing she wasn't allowed to have as a kid. If it wasn't something that fit on a college resume, Tana didn't do it. When she'd left, she decided to change that. She started knitting, crocheting, painting, and had a brief stint with pottery. Her room was covered in random things she'd made and unfinished projects she promised she'd come back to one day.

She turned back to the vanity, taking her hair down. Just that short time up had caused some of her curls to go wonky, and she only had mascara on one eye. All she wanted to do was lay in bed until her shift tomorrow, but she'd promised Bea and she had ditched her one too many times. With a sigh, she got back to getting ready.

2

AMON

Amon snickered when Neil crashed to the floor. He didn't normally cause harm to humans, but watching him try to throw his weight around, acting like a big shot pissed him off. Plus, he only pulled the rug a bit–it's not like he actually pushed him, no matter how much he'd wanted to.

Amon watched as Tana moved back up the stairs with grace. Her hair was tied back, showing off her rounded face. Even though she wore a smile while talking to Neil, Amon could see the irritation burning behind her eyes.

"Hey man, think we'll see a real ghost this time?" one man in Neil's crew asked.

"Probably not," the other replied. "It's not like we've ever seen anything. We'll just shake the camera and shit, slap some scary music in the back and we'll be fine."

Amon rolled his eyes. Amon was *not* a ghost. Ghosts were lost souls that float around, always going nowhere, like they were brain-dead. They weren't even that common. Television always depicted them as being abundant, as if every mundane leftover task people had kept them around.

That wasn't Amon at all; he was a demon who fed off the fear of others.

Most of his kind roamed, causing chaos to feed their magic. Many, many moons ago, Amon was bound to this building. Trapped by a witch who summoned him. Witches called upon his kind for two reasons. Either to trap them and stop them from causing chaos or to help them cause some themselves.

This witch wanted chaos.

Amon refused to help her, and she bound him to this house in anger. He was trapped there and then she sold the place. He became weakened because he wasn't able to feed.

All demons had to eat. Some greed, some anger. Amon fed on fear. Luckily, the house was purchased and he could scare enough people to become more energized. It took some work though. He had no desire to kill anyone, and if he chased out everyone who moved in, the house would sit empty. It was a fine line, but he managed not to scare too many people away and could feed. However, because of the hex, he wasn't able to return to full power. His magic knowledge hadn't been vast to begin with, so he had no way of breaking his hex.

The place was eventually turned into an inn and with the influx of guests, Amon never went hungry. Of course, that sent the human rumor mill spinning and brought assholes like Cornelius to his door. He refused to give idiots like him a show, no matter how tempting the thought of scaring them out the door was.

Amon stalked up the stairway, following Tana. He stepped carefully even though he wasn't really stepping, more floating. He made his way to Tana's room and stood outside the door.

Tana was the most perplexing creature who'd ever

graced these halls. No matter what Amon did, nothing got to her. He'd knocked over her things, moved items to new spots, he'd even opened doors right in front of her. She acted as if nothing happened and moved on. Not a whiff of fear. He'd heard her tell the others she didn't believe in ghosts, so Amon had made it a personal mission to scare her.

Amon solidified his hand and knocked on her door, with three slow, purposeful knocks. He watched as she opened the door, her dark brown eyes staring right through him. Amon took the time to gaze at her. She was smaller than him by more than a foot. Her body was soft and plush, with rounded hips and thick legs. Her warm, chestnut-colored curls cascade to her shoulders, bangs framing her cute round face.

She looked around the hall. Once she noticed no one was there, she shrugged to herself and shut the door without a second thought.

The gall!

Amon was a fearsome demon. If not for this hex he could demolish this entire building with a wave of his hand.

Amon stood there stunned for an unknown amount of time when the door opened again and Tana walked out. She wore a tight pair of jeans and a green top with one sleeve that showed off her belly. She looked pretty. *Really* pretty. If he wasn't invisible, he'd be adjusting himself. She walked through him and out, heading toward the lobby.

"Hello dear. You look nice." An older woman said to Tana.

"Thank you, Mrs. Goldman," Tana replied in that weird voice she used when she talked to guests. Amon had no idea why she did that.

"Of course. I swear a man is going to scoop you up at any moment." The thought of a man scooping Tana up bothered Amon for some reason.

"I don't know about that," Tana answered, which satisfied Amon deeply.

"Well, you have a great time. Tim and I are turning in for the night. We can't be out all night like you kids."

Tana let out a fake laugh. "Alright well, goodnight Mrs. Goldman. See you two tomorrow." When Mrs. Goldman headed up the stairs, Tana dropped the phony smile and continued out the door.

Amon followed her to the porch, watching her get into a car. A woman with long braids sat in the driver's seat, radiating power. She had to be a witch or something. The woman looked at Amon like she could see him, which wasn't possible. At least he didn't think so.

Tana climbed into the car and they drove away. Amon wished he could follow her. The thought was strange and unwelcome, so he shook it off.

On his way up the stairs, he saw the little monster Tana called Binx roaming through the hall. The cat was black and fluffy and seemed to be able to sense his presence, even when he wasn't solid. The thing purred and brushed up against him, but fell right through him. Though the little thing annoyed him greatly he had to admit it was soft.

He checked the hall to make sure no one was coming and solidified his hand, patting its head. It made that vibrating noise that Amon assumed signaled happiness.

He shooed the little fuzz ball away after a few moments. He had more important business to attend to...like scaring the daylights out of the elderly couple in 5E.

3

TANA

Bea and Tana sat in Mel's diner and downed more pancakes and bacon than she thought possible.

"Seee, I told you this was a good idea." Bea slurred. They'd gone out to the bar and gotten slightly sloshed. Even shoving pancakes in her mouth, Beatrix looked gorgeous. She had dark skin that glowed, even under the dull diner lights and long braids that were up in space buns. Her eyes were sharp with glitter falling down from all the movement.

After the bar, Tana had wanted to go straight home, feeling more than partied out. But Bea insisted on going to Mel's first. Apparently, pancakes were the best way to absorb all the alcohol. Tana wasn't sure about that initially, but this *was* a great idea.

"Yes, Bea. This was brilliant," Tana said.

Bea had been one of Tana's closest friends since she moved to Aelmere Heights. Her Nan actually helped Tana get a job at the inn. She and Mrs. Camden were very close. Tana had started as a maid, but Mrs. Camden really liked her and soon she went from maid to desk clerk to manager.

When Mrs. Camden got too old, she taught her the ropes and Tana had been running the show ever since. While it was not what Tana had expected to be doing at this point, she was happy.

"Hey, you think that guy's gonna call?" Bea asked, waggling her brows.

While they were at the bar, some guy came up and bought them drinks while they were playing darts. Tana was sure he was into Bea until he slipped her his number and told her to call.

"Maybe," Tana responded noncommittally. She knew that number would stay buried in the bottom of her bag until she emptied it along with all the other random receipts and wrappers in there. After Courtney, Tana was done with dating.

Courtney and Tana met when Tana first started working at Camden Inn. Courtney was a ghost hunter who was looking for her big break. Courtney and Tana seemed to hit it off instantly, and Tana fell hard. They hooked up and even talked about taking it further.

That was until her husband showed up.

Courtney told him she was sleeping with Tana so she would give her an inside scoop and let her go into restricted areas. She hadn't even believed in ghosts but made up stories to make Courtney happy. She was young and naive and when word got out, Tana was almost fired. Since then she'd sworn off lovers.

Tana had casual hookups when she could, but it was hard when she worked where she lived. Home was also work and she was sure to always remember that. So hookups became few and far between and her vibrator had become her best friend.

"Hey," Bea said, suddenly sounding serious, even

through her drunken haze. "Have you noticed anything strange happening at the inn?"

"What do you mean?" Tana asked.

"Like you know, bumps in the night or anything."

Tana giggled. "Well, we are a haunted inn." She couldn't keep the sarcasm from dripping out. Bea let out a little laugh, but her smile didn't reach her eyes. "Why do you ask?"

She quickly schooled her features. "Oh, nothing. Just curious. I'd heard the place was haunted."

"Supposedly. I think it's all bullshit but what do I know? There's some Neil guy there 'investigating' now." Tana added with air quotes.

"Oh, Neil Cander? isn't he the lead investigator on Ghoul Hunters? I think I've seen it. They've been talking about getting picked up by some TV network"

"Yeah. He's a total prick. He demanded a tour and when I told him no he threw a fit. That was until he tripped on the carpet and fell." Bea laughed mid-sip and spit water everywhere, causing the two to scream and laugh. Luckily, there weren't many other patrons since it was nearly one in the morning.

They finished up their pancakes and called for a cab. Even though the town wasn't big, they lived on opposite sides, so leaving separately seemed to be for the best.

By the time Tana reached the inn, snow had started falling. She knew a blizzard was coming but hoped for a few more days before it started coming down hard. The inn had almost full reservations, and bad weather always meant cancellations.

She paid the cabbie and stepped out, quickly trying to get inside to get warm. Suddenly, there was the crack of a branch behind her, way too close for comfort. Tana turned around, but no one was there. She chalked it up to being too drunk and made her way into the warm inn.

"Hey Tana," Lawrence, the night desk manager, said. He and Tyler were her other managers, along with Diana, who managed housekeeping. She jumped, still slightly tipsy and scared from what had happened outside.

"Woah," he said, putting his arms up. "Sorry, I didn't mean to scare you."

"Oh, it's fine, Lawrence. I'm just a bit jumpy tonight," she told him.

"Understandable, considering all the weird stuff going on lately. Mary Goldman told me someone knocked on her door earlier, but no one was there. She told me if that ghost didn't knock it off, she was gonna exorcize the thing. That woman is hard as nails. And Tyler said he swore he saw someone standing in the woods, but they just vanished before his eyes. Spooky stuff."

Tana hummed, feigning interest. Lawrence was one of her coworkers who actually believed this place was haunted. It was just an old building that made old building noises. Nothing more, nothing less.

"Well, I'm going to bed." She said. But quickly turned back to him. "Oh, by the way, be sure to watch out for that Neil guy. He's some internet ghost hunter who I'm sure is going to try sneaking around."

"Oh, Kaya already filled me in," Lawrence said. "I'll be on the lookout. Have a good night."

"Night Lawrence." She made her way up the stairs, trying to get to her room before anyone saw her.

Once in the room, Tana pet Binx who made herself comfortable on the bed. She then made her way to the bathroom, needing to wash off the lingering smell of beer and peanuts.

After the shower, Tana got in her robe and shuffled to the bedroom to get her makeup remover. She went back to the bathroom and wiped the mirror so she could see. She blinked a few times, her brow furrowing at the strange shadow standing behind her...

A man.

There was a man in her room.

Tana screamed and turned, expecting to see someone standing there, but there was no one. She rechecked the mirror with the same results.

All this talk of ghosts must have been getting to her.

Making her way out of the bathroom, she made sure no one was hiding somewhere else. Once she was sure no one was there, Tana rested in bed, chuckling at herself. She must have let what Lawrence said go to her head. She was drunk and it wouldn't happen again. Figuring she was just paranoid, she drifted off to dream of a tall man standing behind her...but for some reason, she didn't feel afraid.

4

AMON

F*uck.*

Fuck.

That was the only word in Amon's head.

The only word he could use to describe the taste of Tana's fear.

When she finally made it back to the inn, Amon followed her to the door. He stepped on a stick that had been partially buried by the snow, just to see if she might crack, and felt a twinge of something wafting from her. Maybe it was her obvious drunkenness, but he felt like that night he could get to her.

After her conversation with Lawrence, Amon could feel the unease pouring from her. He followed her to her room and waited as she showered. Amon was a lot of things, but a creep wasn't one of them.

When she came to the room in her robe to grab the face wash, he followed behind her, and once she cleared the mirror, he became semi-transparent, making his presence known. She screamed and for the first time, he tasted her fear and *fuck.*

It was the most divine flavor he'd ever tasted. Most fear tasted sort of savory, but hers was sweet. It tasted like honey. He knew he needed more, and he would need to figure out how. He needed to know what made her tick.

He quickly formulated a plan, ready to set it in motion the next day.

THE NEXT DAY, Amon made his way to his personal room, tucked in a hidden entrance in the wall of room 5E. He'd kept all the things he'd gathered over time there. He was very proud of his small treasure trove. It was enough to make a dragon jealous. Not that he'd seen one of those in years.

Amon allowed himself to shift into his normal form. He was seven feet tall, and his skin was red. His horns came from the top of his head, making him appear taller. He'd seen demons with all kinds of horns. Curly and tall, short and thick. His fell somewhere in between. They were medium length and curved at the top, the way those costume devil horns looked.

He'd seen similar depictions of himself in Christian literature about demons. One of the past house owners was extremely religious and had stuff like that all over the place.

While he looked similar, his kind had nothing to do with the Gods, if they even existed. They weren't fallen angels or damned; they were just a species, like any other.

The night before he'd put one of the cellphones he'd taken on a charger so it would be ready for the next day. He dialed the inn's number and waited. Tana was downstairs working, and knowing she was going to answer made him shiver with a strange anticipation.

"Camden Inn, this is Tana."

A shiver ran down Amon's spine. He didn't know why this woman had such an effect on him, but he pushed the thought aside, focusing on his mission.

"Hi," he said casually, "I wanted to see if I could secure a room for a week. I need a room tonight if possible."

"You're in luck. Because of the storm, we've had some cancellations. I just need your full name, email, and phone number." Amon quickly gave her the information. The email was fake, but "Amon Black. Perfect. Just give your name at the desk. We'll see you tonight!" Tana always used that odd voice when she talked to customers, and Amon never knew why. He didn't like when she used it with him

"Perfect. See you then," he said before hanging up. Having everything in place, Amon set out to get his plan into motion. Hopefully, there were some decent clothes left lying around.

5

TANA

"Tan, please don't tell me that was another cancellation," Alise said coming from the kitchen.

She was the chef here at the inn. Alise was shorter than Tana, with long amber hair she kept up most of the time and deep smile lines from constant joy. She smiled more than anyone Tana knew. Alise had planned for a full house for the next few days even though Tana told her to plan for some of these cancellations, but the idea of not having enough food to feed everyone twice over made her hyperventilate.

"No, actually," Tana said, "it was a man making a reservation for tonight."

"Oh goodie. Is his wife coming? I need people to feed."

"No, it's just him." Tana could feel Alise's eyes on her.

"A man coming to an inn alone," Alise said, looking thoughtful. "That's an interesting choice."

"I guess." Tana tried not to think about why guests were there. After what happened with Courtney, she had no interest in the guests' personal lives.

"Hm. Well, it doesn't matter. I hope he's hungry. And hey, maybe he's cute and single. Oh! That would be such a meet-cute moment for you Tan. And who doesn't love that?" Between her and Bea, Tana felt like she would never get peace.

"You know I'm not interested in dating right now," she said.

"I know," Alise said, "but fate does what fate does."

Tana rolled her eyes at that. She wasn't so sure about fate. It hadn't seemed to do her any favors thus far, and she didn't want to start expecting things now.

After that, the day seemed to fly by. One of the maids had called out so Tana ended up doing some cleaning around the inn. The snow seemed endless and had to be shoveled constantly. Most other guests had also canceled, so only Neil and his crew and this new guest would be there. Everyone else had left the day before. Even the Goldmans left early–who, despite their age came here often, loving the good scare they got.

Tana finally made it back to the desk that evening. She continued crocheting a rug she'd started when the door opened and a man who she assumed to be their other guest walked in.

He had bright red hair that must have been dyed and was at least six feet tall. He wasn't super muscular, but he was toned, with eyes so dark they seemed almost black and sharp features. His pale skin glowed against the beaming white snow outside, like a halo of light surrounding him.

"Hi, welcome to the Camden Inn," Tana said, in her best customer service voice. "You must be who called this morning."

"Yes, Amon," he said, reaching his hand out. She took it,

noticing how warm his hands were, despite the frigid cold he'd just come from.

"Amazing, welcome in. I hope your trip wasn't too bad. It's really coming down out there."

"It wasn't too bad. I was already close by."

"Good, well, let's get you checked in." Tana got through the check-in process quickly. It was second nature to her at this point. Normally, that made her job easier, but now it gave her way too much brain space to stare at Amon.

They were halfway through the process when she heard talking coming from the stairs.

"And now we're heading into the lobby," Neil said, followed by his crew recording. "Some say a man tripped and fell on a pen here on these very stairs, stabbing himself in the eye. People claim to have seen a one-eyed apparition moving around this space." After that little intro, he stopped talking and the man in front of him lowered his camera.

Tana watched in amusement. A man stabbing himself with a pen? Really? That was the most ridiculous story she'd ever heard. Amon raised his eyebrows at her in question.

"Oh, this place is super haunted," Tana informed him, struggling to keep the sarcasm out of her voice.

"Really?" Amon asked.

"Yes, very. You know, misplaced items, things moving on their own, apparitions. The whole shebang. I'm surprised you didn't know that. It's the reason a lot of people come here."

"And do you believe it?"

She thought for a moment. "I've heard so many stories it seems like they couldn't *all* be fabricated."

Tana normally lied right through her teeth to guests, but she couldn't seem to lie to him. She did choose her words wisely, however, sure to keep her tone light. You never know who's a crazy ghost enthusiast in disguise. Tana had had guests lie about not knowing there was a ghost just to try to get the staff to tell more stories, even though Tana had none.

"Sounds like bullshit to me. But what do I know?" Amon said with a shrug.

They watched as Neil and his crew moved around the space, getting shots of the room.

"Ah, hello Taylor," Neil said when he noticed they were paying attention. "How are you?"

"Just fine Neil," she said, ignoring the incorrect name she was called, "how's your filming going?"

"Amazing. This place really is the real deal. We've already caught a few orbs floating around and heard some bumping around in the middle of the night."

"Of course," Tana said on reflex. She'd heard this term before. It was ghost hunter speak for flecks of dust floating around in the camera. "I've lived here for years and have my fair share of stories."

Amon eyed her, making her feel uneasy, as if he could see right through her shit.

"Yes, well. We're just doing some B-roll if you don't mind. Nothing you say would be in the recording. However, it would be amazing if I could interview you for the video. I think with the amount of footage we have, we could do a three-part series."

Tana clenched her jaw, trying not to show her displeasure. She didn't want to be a part of this ongoing narrative. "Oh, I'm not sure. I'm actually planning on going out-of-town tomorrow to my parents for the holidays."

"You're leaving?" Amon asked.

"That's the plan," she told him. His expression changed momentarily, but she barely caught it before it was gone.

"Well, that's a shame," Neil chimed in, "maybe some of the other staff would want an interview?"

"You're free to ask," she told him, even though she didn't think anyone would go for it. Lawrence was the only one who really believed any of the ghost stuff, but he'd turned guys like this down before. Said he didn't like the attention.

Neil nodded and went back to his crew. Tana finished checking Amon in, gave him his key, and directed him to his room. He said his thanks and took his leave. Tana hunkered back down with her rug, watching the snow continue to come down outside.

THE NEXT DAY, Tana gathered the last of her clothes to take to her parents. Binx crawled up and laid in her suitcase.

"You're not coming," she told the cat. Binx didn't seem interested in that answer, however, going back to laying in the top of the case.

There was a knock on her door. Tana put her clothes down and moved to open it. "Hey Tan," Kaya said when she opened the door. She had her 'I have bad news' face plastered on.

"What's up Kay?" Tana asked.

"So I just got off the phone with Harold, the plow guy. He said there was no way anyone was making it on or off this drive."

Tana's heart sank. "What?"

"Yeah, he said the plows were getting stuck on their way here so they couldn't continue," Kaya said. "All the roads are blocked until the snow stops."

"Shit." Tana took a second to think. "Okay, Kay, you go

down and call everyone who hasn't canceled and let them know. I'll talk to our current guests and let them know."

"Rodger," she said with a mock salute before running down the hall.

First, Tana grabbed her phone to tell her parents she wasn't going to make it.

"What do you mean you're not coming home?" her mom cried over the phone. "Everyone's coming. Just hop in your car and come."

"I can't, mom. The roads are completely blocked. Plus, now we're short-staffed because no one can come in or out. I need to be here."

"You know, you could be doing a lot more than managing some mom-and-pop inn. Then you wouldn't be stuck there."

Tana rolled her eyes. They had this conversation often and Tana didn't have time for it. "Well, it is what I do. And right now, I need to be here. I'll call when the snow clears up."

"Fine, fine. I'll let your father know. I hope you can join us for Christmas. We rarely see you anymore."

I wonder why, Tana thought. But she promised to try and said her goodbyes. With that squared away, she pet Binx on the head one last time and focused on the inn.

Tana went to Neil's room first. She knocked, waiting for him to open up. After a few moments of silence, she was was worried he wasn't there. Finally she heard a thud behind the door. When it opened, it was a man from Neil's crew. "Sup?" he said.

"Hi," Tana said. "So we just wanted to inform you that due to the snowstorm the roads are completely blocked. No one can come in or go out."

"Till when?" She heard Neil yell from in the room. He

came to the door, replacing the other man. His brown hair was perfectly groomed and his flannel looked ironed. It was like he was never anything but perfect.

"The plow guys weren't sure, but they said they'd call. The storm is supposed to last for a few days, but if it lightens up the plows should be able to make it."

Neil ran a hand over his face. "Fine, whatever. Brian!" he called back to the room, she assumed at one of the other guys. "Call Terry and let him know. We'll stay here, do some more filming. Make this some sort of series."

Turning his attention back to Tana, he said, "so, now we're all on lockdown, you think you'd want to do that interview?"

"Uh, maybe. There's a lot to do, but I'll get back to you." Tana had absolutely no plans on doing that interview, but it was best to use her customer service voice with guys like this.

He nodded, eying her up and down. "Well, maybe we could do just a one-on-one interview. It may make you more comfortable."

Tana hummed noncommittally. There was no way she wanted to do whatever he was implying. With that maybe, Neil went back to his room.

Next was Amon. She knocked and he answered quickly. When she went through her whole snowed-in spiel, he looked amused, like some joke she wasn't a part of.

"No problem," he said in that deep baritone voice of his. "I'm here on vacation anyway, so no plans are interrupted."

"You decided to vacation at an inn by yourself in the middle of winter?" Tana normally wouldn't pry like this, but for some reason, she couldn't help herself. "You ski or something?"

"I quite like the winter," he said. He crossed his arms and

leaned against the doorframe. "Plus, this place has a certain charm to it. I had to come to find out for myself."

"Right," she said, dragging out the vowel and frowning. She wasn't quite convinced. "Well, anyway, all meals will be served downstairs at their normal times. Let us know if you need anything."

"Sure thing," he said with a wink.

Normally, her stomach turned when guests did things like that. But when Amon did it, she felt herself melt a bit. He closed the door and She turned on her heel, headed to the front desk. She needed to call Mrs. Camden. Even though she was very hands-off, she still liked to be updated about things like this.

"Oh Tan, have you heard?" Alise called as Tana entered.

"Yes Alise, I just informed the guests. Are you guys gonna be okay here?" she asked Kaya and Alise. They didn't live in the inn. Kaya assured them her classes were over for the semester and she planned to work anyway and Alise had already called her husband to let him know. Lawrence was upstairs sleeping since he lived at the inn as well. She would have to catch up with him later.

"You both are welcome to a room, we have plenty. We need to make sure guests are staying entertained and fed."

"Food is covered," Alise said. "I've got enough food to feed everyone for weeks."

"We know," Tana and Kaya said at the same time.

"I'm sure Neil and his crew will keep themselves busy, we just need to be sure they stay out of trouble," Tana said. "And Amon seemed content when I talked to him, so I think he's fine."

"I'll say," Alise murmured under her breath. "I'd love to take a bite out of that snack."

Tana's eyes widened and moved to the stairs, making

sure Amon wasn't standing there. "Alise!" she exclaimed. "He's a guest."

"Yes, and I'm a person with eyes. And taste."

Kaya giggled and Tana couldn't help joining in. He really was something.

Yeah," Kaya said, "Even I think so, and I don't like men."

Tana rolled her eyes, though she was still grinning. She couldn't believe these two.

"Come on," Tana said. "We have work to do." The two mock straightened and saluted, causing them all to giggle.

They all started walking away when Alise turned back around, moving in close. "Don't fight fate, Tan. Especially when it comes in that sexy of a package." With that, she went back to the kitchen. Tana thought about it for a moment and then let it go.

What did fate know anyway?

6

AMON

Amon waited for Tana to leave and went to his actual room. Now he was here, he realized he hadn't thought very far ahead. He was here, visible to her.

Now what?

He'd never been around Tana in a way she could acknowledge him. He'd always been ghostly and had only been around people a handful of other times. Amon spoke with a passing demon once about twenty years ago. He sympathized with Amon's predicament and told him if he found anything out, he would come back and help.

Amon hadn't seen him since.

He used to entertain himself by pretending to be the mailman before it was an inn. The mailman assumed he was the one who lived there and would give him their packages. He often talked to the owners.

They even gave him cookies once during the holidays since they assumed he was their mailman. When he stopped coming and the real mailman showed up, the fear of who this random man was kept him fed for a long time.

Other than those incidents, which were few and far between in the grand scheme of things, Amon rarely interacted with anyone directly. Just watched. Hence why this plan was suddenly feeling foolish. He was just glad words were coming out of his mouth at all when Tana was around.

Also, now that he could be around her physically, he noticed the taste of her fear was like a constant, sweet scent, that drove him crazy. She smelled like those cookies he'd been given. The woman had called them sugar cookies. Her scent was nowhere near as strong and wasn't at all filling, but that enticing flavor remained, and he had no idea why. He wished he had someone to ask, but who would he? At least the snowstorm kept her here. He thought all his plans were dashed when she said she planned on leaving the day before.

He suddenly remembered she had said something about food. It would probably be very odd if he never went to eat.

He concentrated and morphed back into his human skin to make his way downstairs. Looking in the mirror again, he couldn't help but stare at this strange form. His previously crimson skin was now creamy and his horns were gone. His hair was red like his skin once was, but his eyes remained dark. Not to mention his now missing tail.

Amon left his room, feeling a bit self-conscious. He had never been self-conscious until this moment, but with Tana able to see him, he became acutely aware of what he looked like. He wanted to impress her. To make it clear that he was someone worth spending time with.

He made his way into the dining room. Kaya had given him a small wave when he passed and he waved back.

Good start.

When Amon got there, he was pleasantly surprised Neil was no where to be found. The thought of him flirting with

Tana again set him on edge, even though she seemed very uninterested.

The dining room looked just like the rest of the inn. The walls were covered in a cream wallpaper with golden filigree and the furniture was vintage and all mismatched.

When this place first became an inn, it was about 1970 and the new owners found all the furniture that had been left to rot in the attic. They had refurbished a lot of it and he could see some of it here again, mixed in with newer additions. It should have been cozy and warm, especially with the snow coming down outside, but to Amon, it just felt like a prison.

"Oh, hey doll, you hungry?" Alise asked, coming through the kitchen.

He knew she was the cook here. She'd been here for a very long time and from what Amon understood, she made excellent food. He hadn't eaten real food in years. It wasn't that he couldn't, but he didn't need to.

"Yes please," he told her.

"Oh, what manners. Not like that ghost-hunting crew," He gave her a polite smile and nod but wasn't sure what else to say. "Well, you sit down and I'll get you something for lunch. Maybe a club sandwich, or a wrap. Oh, dear, you're not a vegetarian are you?"

"No."

"Perfect." She turned to hustle back to the kitchen but managed to trip on what seemed like thin air. Amon rushed over to help her up.

"Are you alright?" he asked once she was righted again.

"Yeah, yeah. I'm just a mighty fine clutz." She ran her hands down her front, straightening her clothes.

"What happened?" he heard Tana approach. She stepped through the swinging door from the kitchen.

Her curly, dark hair was tied up in a knot. Her front was wet, and she had gloves on, like she'd been washing dishes.

"Oh nothin' Tan," Alise said. "I just took a tumble."

"You've got to stop doing that. You'll send me to an early grave." Tana helped Alise to the kitchen while fretting over her, much to Alise's annoyance.

Once she got Alise squared away, she came back out. "Thanks for helping her out. I love Alise, but she's a bit of a klutz."

"Well, then I guess it's a good thing she works with knives all day long," Amon said dryly.

Tana huffed a laugh, giving the impression there had been an accident or two before. Amon spent little time in the kitchen. Scaring people with knives never seemed like a good idea.

"Just to warn you, Alise is probably going to make you everything in the kitchen. She planned for double the guests and feels the need to feed everyone till they're rolling out of here." He noticed she didn't use that false, high-pitched voice she used with other customers, which pleased him.

"That's fine, I'm famished," Amon lied. He didn't get hungry per se, but when he hadn't been consuming fear and using his magic, he felt weak. He knew this was something people said, however.

"Yeah, me too," she said. Did humans feel weak when they were hungry? He'd seen his share of humans that became irrationally angry, and then later blamed it on hunger. Would Tana do that?

Humans were strange.

Alise came back holding two plates in her hands. She set one in front of him and the other in front of Tana.

"Oh Ali," Tana said, "You didn't need to make me anything."

"Nonsense," Alise replied. "You need to eat. You've been running around all day and I'm sure you haven't had anything but coffee today."

Tana shrugged. Amon felt a twinge of worry thinking about Tana not taking care of herself. She seemed healthy, but when he looked closer, he noticed the bags under her eyes and exhaustion marring her features.

"Well, you should eat with me then?" he said, coming out more like a question.

"Well, if you're sure. Alise, I'll come back to the kitchen to help finish up the dishes soon."

"No problem dear, take your time." Alise disappeared back to the kitchen, leaving them alone.

Amon looked to his plate where a grilled chicken and bacon sandwich, fries, and a side salad awaited him. "Wow, you weren't kidding about the amount of food."

"Nope," Tana said, popping the 'P' loudly. "Good thing Ali is the best chef ever." After eating a few bites, Amon had to agree. He hadn't eaten too much human food in his life, but this simple sandwich was excellent.

They ate their food in relative silence. It wasn't uncomfortable, but Amon wished to talk with her more, and he didn't know what to say.

"So, vacationing at an inn huh?" Tana asked, finally breaking the silence.

"Yes," Amon said. Tana had made a similar comment when they were talking earlier. She looked amused, but he wasn't sure why. All he'd done was answer her question.

"May I ask why?" she asked.

"Why?"

"Yeah. It just seems like a strange place to vacation alone. And it's not like we're in a vibrant town or anything."

That was true. Amon hadn't been into the town in almost a century, but even back then it was small.

"Um. I just wanted to try something new." It wasn't quite a lie.

"You from the city or something?"

"Or something," he responded. She laughed, which made him smile too.

"Well," Tana said, standing. "I guess I should get back to work. You would be surprised how much four men will eat."

"You mean Neil and his crew?" Amon asked, trying to keep the venom from his voice. He wasn't fond of being referred to as a ghost, nor was he fond of Neil openly flirting with Tana.

"Yep. There are only four of us here, so we've all been chipping in. Luckily it's only you and them."

Amon nodded, not quite sure what else to say. She grabbed his plate and returned to the kitchen. He sat and stared at the door she just disappeared behind. Amon wasn't sure why but he wanted to follow. He ignored the pull and went back to his room, determined to get closer to her.

Somehow.

7

TANA

Tana sat at the desk, reading a book she found on one of the shelves. She wasn't much of a reader, but she had to unravel about half of her rug earlier when she realized she accidentally skipped a stitch in the middle. Frustrated, she set the project aside and decided to do something else. Since she couldn't get to the craft store, and all of the other half-finished projects didn't seem appealing, books it was.

It was only eight AM, and she'd already had a conversation with the plow guy who still had nothing new, and spoke with Mrs. Camden again, assuring her everything was being taken care of.

Lawrence was sleeping on the desk when she got here this morning, and she couldn't blame him. She helped him back to his room and got to business. Once Kay was there, she would need to do the laundry, check on Alise, and do some more shoveling. Lawrence had done most of it, but she wanted to give him a break.

"You know, that book is awful," a deep voice said, cutting through her thoughts. Amon hovered above her, leaning over the desk. His unnaturally red hair fell around his face. It was messy, but matched him.

She wasn't even paying attention to the book at that point; she just needed the distraction.

"Well, I think it's pretty interesting," Tana said, trying to get a rise out of him.

"That would make you wrong." He leaned in further, tipping the book down so he could gauge how far she was.

"You've barely broken into the first chapter. Trust me, that's a blessing." With him this close, she noticed he smelled like smoke, cedar, and something sweet she couldn't place. Maybe it was some fancy cologne. Or maybe he just smelled like that?

"Well, it's a good first chapter," she responded instead of commenting on his scent like her brain wanted her to.

He hummed in disagreement and stood up, taking his lush scent with him. It bothered her. She wished he would lean in again, and the thought was alarming. She'd never just wanted to smell someone before, and she didn't plan on starting now.

"You don't read enough good books then," he said.

"I rarely read. It's not really my thing." When Tana was young, reading was one of the approved hobbies she could have. Of course, between the chess team, dance lessons, and the after-school study groups, she was too exhausted to do much of anything else. Plus, she preferred things that kept her hands busy.

"Well, I can recommend some better ones."

Amon walked over to the small reading room off the edge of the lobby. Tana closed the book, watching him walk off. She heard rustling and shuffling until he came back with a pretty significant stack.

He dropped them on the desk with a loud smack. The stack towered over her, just short of fully blocking Amon.

"These are some of the best," he said matter-of-factly.

Tana perused the stack. Some of the books were older, with cracked spines and worn titles; while some were newer, obviously left from guests on their travels.

"This one," he said, holding up a yellow book, "is a great mystery novel. I won't spoil it, but the twist was really good. And this one is an excellent horror. Had me up for days."

Tana listened as he told her about each book, Even though books weren't her thing, watching Amon excitedly explain them all made her want to devour the stack. This was the first time he didn't seem nervous while talking to her and she loved this side of him.

Once he was finished, he looked at her expectantly. She considered all of his descriptions and picked up the mystery he'd initially talked about and a rom-com he'd explained was truly funny.

"Great choices," he said as he pushed the stacks to the end of the desk and leaned over, wafting his scent at her.

She unconsciously leaned forward, inhaling his scent. Even though he was tall, with him leaning over, they were practically face to face. His eyes were sharp and assessing. It felt as if he were looking *through* her. It should have made her feel uncomfortable, but for the first time in a long time, she felt...seen.

"Oh, Tan, there you are!" Alise's voice called, breaking the spell. They pulled away and Amon looked as embarrassed as she felt.

Alise had a knowing smile on her face that Tana promptly ignored. "Yes Ali, what is it?"

"Oh, right. I was wondering if you could help with some

of the kitchen prep. I just want to be sure everything gets done."

"Sure. Kay said she was gonna come back around noon, so I'll come then."

Alise nodded and disappeared to the kitchen, leaving her and Amon alone. "Well. I should probably..." Tana trailed off.

Amon's eyes widened. "Oh. Yes. Of course. I should go... enjoy vacation."

Tana laughed at that and Amon left, heading back up the stairs. She watched him until the phone rang, dragging Tana from all thoughts of Amon and his smoky scent.

Why did he smell so good?

And why did it feel like she'd experienced that scent before?

8

TANA

Tana was over this snow. It just wouldn't stop piling up, covering the world in a harsh white light.

To make matters worse, it kept Neil and his annoying crew here longer. She'd been trying to monitor them, but with only a few staff here and so much to do, it was becoming more challenging.

Just the other night Lawrence said he saw one of them trying to sneak down to the basement, but he managed to catch him first. If one of them got injured, it would be on Tana's shoulders, and she wasn't about to let that happen. As much as she complained, Tana loved the inn and wanted to continue working there.

Neil also continued to ask her for an interview, refusing to get the hint. She did like having Amon here. She hadn't had the chance to read any of the books yet, but every time she looked at them, she thought about his dark eyes and strange conversational skills.

Pushing those thoughts away, Tana stood outside of Neil's door for a minute. All the maids were out due to the storm, and with Kay working the desk, Alise in the kitchen, and Lawerence getting some sleep, Tana had to clean the rooms. She didn't mind; it was sort of relaxing. A consistent routine. However, she had no intention of being cornered by Neil for an interview, or anything else.

She heard them walking around in there and quickly walked away.

Nope.

She made her way to empty rooms, turning the beds down. She knew she was avoiding the inevitable, but sometimes ignorance was bliss.

When there was only one place left to go, Tana made her way to Amon's door. She told herself he was just another guest. Whether he gave her butterflies or not.

When she got there, she knocked and waited. There was no noise on the other side of the door. She was about to get the key, assuming he was out, when the door swung open with no one was there. She rolled her eyes.

Stupid old door latch.

Tana rolled her cart in and started cleaning. Every room was the same, so it never felt invasive. But for some reason, access to Amon's room felt invasive. They'd had a few... moments, but that didn't mean anything. Tana was sticking to her guns. No relationship with a guest could work out.

Plus, he had a life somewhere far away from here that Tana would never be a part of. Tana thought of him in an office in some big city. He probably lived on the top floor of a crazy tall skyscraper with a pool in it or something.

Even with all this logic in her head, she still kicked the suitcase open while walking by.

"Oops," she said out loud, like someone else was there. Looking inside, she saw some clothes sitting on the top and that was basically it. Since she'd already opened her box of crazy, Tana opened the drawers to the nightstands against the bed. No sign of a hidden wedding ring or photos of kids.

Tana was checking the other one when she heard someone clearing their throat behind her.

She jumped, feeling fear rush through her. Tana slammed the drawer and turned to see Amon there. He was leaning against the door looking right at her.

"Hi there," he said casually.

"Uh, hi. I was just...cleaning." She knew it sounded lame, but what was she supposed to say?

"The drawer?" he asked.

"Yup. full turn down and everything." She widened her smile, trying to sell the obvious lie.

"Interesting." He moved closer to her, and her heartbeat rose, a shiver running down her spine. "Did you find what you were looking for?"

"No...I wasn't...I mean, -"

He tipped her chin up so they were eye to eye. The words faded from her lips. Silence filled the space. The only sound was her heart thudding in her chest. He leaned in further, their lips almost touching.

"You could just ask, snow bunny. I would tell you anything you wanted to know." She didn't know where the nickname came from, but her brain was too scattered to dwell on it. She wanted to kiss him, but could feel her anxiety rising. Memories of Courtney flooded back.

"I—I have to go." She rushed around him to the cart, pushing it as quickly as she could down the hall and away from Amon.

Relationships with guests never worked out; she *had* to remember that.

And more than anything, she had to shovel her way out of this inn.

9

AMON

Amon watched Tana as she threw another mound of snow up over the railing. She'd been out there for an hour and had only shoveled half the porch. Since their incident in his room yesterday, she was avoiding him. Amon saw her in the dining room earlier that morning, but she just blushed and ran back to the kitchen.

When she'd come to the room yesterday, he decided to try and give her another scare. He opened the locked door right in front of her but she didn't even flinch. Most people would have keeled over.

The day before he knocked over one of the ghost hunter's Axe body spray can and he squealed like a girl. That particular feeding felt good.

It occurred to him while watching her that she was looking for something. But what? She didn't even think ghosts were real, so Amon didn't think she suspected him. He decided to go for a new tactic and solidified. She seemed much more frightened by actual people than ghosts.

Amon honestly couldn't blame her.

Her fear was delicious. Even though it quickly changed

to embarrassment and shame. Amon didn't want her to feel this way, nor did he understand why she did. Amon wanted her to tell him what was wrong, wanted to reassure her. But being that close made him want...*more.*

But then she ran, and Amon could do nothing but stand there.

So now he watched her out the window, trying to give her the space she seemed to want. Was she planning on shoveling the whole thing? He could easily clear all that snow with a flick of his wrist, but that may raise the wrong types of questions.

He made his way downstairs, eager to corner her. After she visited his room yesterday, he knew he needed more. Making a quick stop by the kitchen, he asked Alise to whip up her favorite hot drink.

"How sweet," Alise cooed when he asked.

She handed him two drinks that smelled of chocolate and peppermint and he headed out the door. When he got there, he wasn't sure what he was looking at.

Tana swung her shovel at the pile of snow, yelling in anger. "Stupid, stupid snow," she shouted. "Stupid. No. Awning. Porch."

He just watched for a moment, taking in the scene.

"Did it steal your wallet or something, snow bunny?" he finally asked.

She whipped around and he noticed her face was flushed and her golden brown eyes were wide with surprise. Her unruly curls were barely contained under a deep blue beanie. The matching puffer jacket she had was now equally ruffled and covered in snow.

She chucked the shovel down and wiped a gloved hand across her forehead. "It might as well have," she said with a huff of amusement. "Wait. What did you just call me?"

"Well, you are hopping around the snow like a bunny so." Amon shrugged. He had called her the same thing yesterday, but then she was too distracted to notice.

Tana plopped down on the bench she'd cleared, seeming to let it go. Amon quickly joined her, careful not to spill the mugs in his hands. The bench was cold and the leftover snow began to soak through his jeans.

Amon offered her the drink, and she took it happily.

"Ahhh," she said, as she sipped it, "my favorite, thanks."

"Well, I can't take all the credit. Alise made it."

"Still, you didn't have to."

He shrugged. "So, can I ask what the snow did to deserve such treatment?"

"Other than existing...nothing I guess," she sighed. "I just got a bit frustrated with everything going on."

"Neil?"

"Neil. The plow guy. Mrs. Camden. My parents. The list is endless at this point." He wanted her to elaborate, but decided not to push after what happened yesterday. He just nodded instead.

Luckily, she kept going. "I mean, I'm only one person. I can't update Mrs. Camden every five minutes and watch the crazy ghost people, and help in the kitchen and shovel the driveway. Maybe my parents were right. Maybe I should have just gone to college, found a husband, and had kids. That's what everyone else did. And they are all in their warm homes, baking cookies or some shit. While I'm here shoveling this porch. Freezing my ass off."

Amon tried to absorb all of this and tried to find the right words. "Do you like baking?"

Tana huffed. "What?"

"I mean. That sounds nice if you like baking and kids.

But if you don't, maybe even if you were warm and comfortable, you might not be...happy."

Tana sat there silently for a moment. "You're right. I would be miserable. The holidays always bring this out of me. It's the only time I have to go home and deal with it." She peered over at him. "I'm sorry. I barely know you and here I am, trauma dumping all over you."

"It's okay. You may dump on me whenever you like."

She laughed and went back to looking off the porch, seeming lost in thought. He sipped his drink and found it way too sweet. The mint was nice, but this drink could definitely rot your teeth.

"Not a fan of peppermint hot chocolate?" she asked as she watched him make a face.

"It's too sweet," he tells her.

"That's the best part!" she exclaims. He disagreed but was glad her smile was back.

Their eyes met and her face seemed to get even redder than it was before.

Suddenly, a crash sounded from the shed on the other side of the lawn. They both hopped up and headed toward the sound. Tana plodded through the snow, even though it was almost to her knees.

When they got there, Neil and his crew were helping one of their members out from under a stack of plywood.

"What are you doing?" Tana said, voice tight with anger.

Neil whipped around to see them both standing there.

"Hey Tasha," he said, with his greasy smirk. "We were just trying to get some extra shots and Josh here slipped."

Tana crossed her arms. "I'm pretty sure we've discussed that you aren't allowed in restricted areas. Get your friends and get out of here please."

"It was an accident." Neil defended. "Maybe we could

work something out. Perhaps you could give me a private tour instead."

He took a step toward her, but Amon moved quicker, blocking his path. Anger seethed under Amon's skin; he didn't want this slimy human touching her.

"I'm pretty sure she was clear about you getting the fuck out," Amon said.

Neil's smirk quickly dissolved into anger. He looked Amon up and down. "I don't know who you are, but we're done here."

Neil tried to sidestep him, but Amon was faster. He pushed Neil back against the wall, using his forearm to pin him in place. Neil struggled a bit but was no match for Amon's strength. Amon was ready to crush him.

He'd never felt the anger his kind normally succumbed to, but now he could feel it bubbling under his skin, threatening to erupt.

"Amon," Tana called, cutting through his angry thoughts. Then she was pulling on him and he allowed her to, releasing Neil.

"Clean this up and go inside," she told them. "Lawerence will be out to check you're gone." Without stopping, she dragged him up the stairs and down the hall to her room.

He could feel the fear rolling off her in waves. And even though it had the most delicious taste, Amon didn't feel good about it.

10

TANA

H*oly shit.*

She led Amon into her space and quickly shut the door. He stood in the middle of her room, seeming unsure where to look. She didn't know why they were here either. Neil made her so mad, but the look on Amon's face made her scared. Not of him exactly, but of what he was about to do to Neil. Something in his eyes changed, like he was turning into someone Tana didn't recognize.

"I scared you," Amon said, breaking the silence. He sounded almost defeated, with his gaze cast to the ground.

She took a deep breath. "No. No, I just didn't want things to escalate."

"So...you aren't scared of me?"

"No," she said, which was the truth. She couldn't explain it, but Amon made her feel comfortable. Safe. Tana also couldn't explain why she brought him here in the first place. She just got anxious about him hurting Neil and knew she needed to get him out of there.

She never brought anyone to her room. Not since Courtney. Looking around, she took notice of all her clothes on the floor and plies of unfinished crafts and tried not to feel self-conscious. Binx appeared from under her bed and began purring like a motorboat. She rubbed against Amon. While he looked slightly annoyed, he did lean down and pat her head.

"That's Binx." Tana said. "And I think she likes you"

"I don't know why. Animals normally don't like me."

Amon stood back up and met her eyes. His gaze was heated, surely matching hers. After a few more breaths, he stepped forward. They were now inches apart. His eyes flickered with an emotion she didn't expect and refused to think about.

Tana reached for him and they met in a tangle of limbs. She didn't know who went in first, but when their lips touched, it was electric. His smoke and cedar smell invaded her senses, making her melt.

He slid his tongue into her mouth, dominating the kiss. He tasted of peppermint hot chocolate and something else uniquely his. Her body was on fire pressed to his. Amon groaned into her mouth, and she sighed in return.

The kiss lasted for what felt like forever, but at the same time, only moments. He pulled away and started unzipping her jacket. It fell to the floor with a thud and she quickly slid out of her boots. They broke the kiss while he removed his coat and boots. When they reconnected, he led her to the bed.

When he laid her down, she quickly pulled him closer, feeling a bit impatient. He huffed a laugh, but came down, meeting her kiss. He trailed kisses down her jaw, leading to her neck. His lips were soft as they trailed lower, reaching her collarbone. He pulled away and met her gaze. She could tell he wanted permission to continue.

Tana nodded. "Yes," she breathed, giving him the reassurance he asked for.

He stripped her of her shirt and pants at an almost inhuman speed, leaving her bare except for her panties.

Amon groaned as he took her in. Normally, sex wasn't like this. It was about getting in, getting off, and getting out. Even with Courtney, it felt like passion in the moment, but it was just a means to an end.

Now, Amon just hovered above her, staring as if he was cataloging every inch of her. Instead of being self-conscious, she basked in the attention.

Tana moaned, rubbing her thighs together, trying to rid herself of the tension building in her core.

"Need some help there, snow bunny?" he asked, eyes traveling lower.

"Please," she hissed out desperately. She had never been this needy before.

All amusement left his face as he sprang into action. He brought his lips to her nipple, his hands trailing down her body. Tana's body broke out in goosebumps as his hands dragged down her stomach to her thighs.

He squeezed her ass and growled against her nipple. When his mouth shifted to give the other nipple attention, his hand found its mark, swirling against her clit.

She cried out, relieved to finally have some friction. Tana rode against him, chasing her relief. His mouth soon trailed lower, kissing down her stomach to her lower belly. Her body felt like it was on fire. His fingers were soon replaced with the flat of his tongue.

"Fuck, snow bunny," he said, voice hoarse, "you taste so good." He dipped his finger inside and she cried out. "So good and wet for me," he said, continuing to lick and suck.

She was so close. Tana rode his face, grinding hard against him. Pleasure hit her like a wave, causing her thighs to shake and her brain to melt. Amon continued licking and sucking her through her orgasm, only stopping when she came down, like he knew she was too sensitive.

He kissed his way back up her body, and she met him with lazy, drawn-out kisses. She could taste herself along with him and it was exhilarating.

Tana sat up, realizing she didn't return the favor. "Do you want me to -?"

"No, bunny," he said, cutting her off and dragging her back to him.

"But -"

"No buts. Well, only this one," he said as he squeezed her backside. Tana laughed and settled back down, wrapping herself in his arms. She felt a twinge of disappointment, but didn't dwell on it for too long. She would be worried he wasn't attracted to her if it wasn't for the electric energy between them.

Plus the giant hardness she felt resting against her thigh.

Amon ran his fingers through her hair, getting caught in her curls. "If you do that, you'll ruin all my curls," she said with fake annoyance.

"Really?" he asked skeptically.

"Yes. If I were to brush this all out, it'd look like I was electrocuted."

"Oh, I have to see that."

She gave him a playful shove and he laughed, not budging an inch. He wasn't particularly large, but he was dense.

She wanted more, but she was suddenly exhausted–
entirely drained after he made her come. They lay in bed,
talking about nothing until her eyes fluttered shut. And
when she drifted off, content in his arms, she knew there
was so much more to come.

11

AMON

A mon watched Tana sleep, mesmerized by her relaxed nature. He thought he had royally screwed up earlier when he tasted the fear wafting off of her. His anger overtook him and, if he was honest with himself, he wasn't sure what he would have done.

But when they got back to the room, and she looked at him with that heated gaze, it was all over. Amon was sure he took the first step, but she met him instantly, until they were nothing more than a tangle of limbs and kisses.

And her *taste*. She tasted like heaven–that was the only way to describe it. It was like her fear concentrated. He didn't think he would ever get enough. She'd wanted to continue, but he didn't feel right. Even though he looked human, he wasn't, and something about continuing without her knowing unsettled him. Plus, his cock didn't change, and she would for sure notice it wasn't quite the same.

None of it made sense. Sure, Tana was gorgeous, smart, and funny, but he felt so protective over her. Even though she had thoroughly proved she could take care of herself.

He wished he had someone else to ask about what was going on with him. With her.

But he pushed those thoughts aside. Right now, something else was still bothering him.

Or should he say, *someone*.

And that someone was easy to take care of. He stared at Tana's sleeping form for another moment before kissing her forehead and standing, turning invisible. Binx was laying by the fireplace, now with only a few embers burning. He patted her on the head, to her annoyance, and continued on his mission.

As he made his way down the stairs, he saw the tail end of one of Neil's men slipping down to the basement.

Typical.

He slid to the basement to find all the guys huddled around, setting up ghost-hunting equipment.

"Dude, are you sure we won't get in trouble? The manager lady already yelled at us once today," one of them said.

"Kyle, you have to chill out," Neil said. "Even if we get caught, I'll just talk us out of it. That Taryn girl is basically in love with me. I'll just sweet-talk her again. I was thinking of getting in her pants anyway. She's alright looking. Plus, maybe she'll spill some inside info."

Anger bubbled in Amon's chest. *Tana* wouldn't give him the time of day if he wasn't a guest.

Plus, he wasn't the one with her taste still on his tongue.

He watched as the guys finished setting up and started recording.

"Welcome to the basement," Neil stage whispered to the camera. "It's said a woman tripped and died on these very stairs. Could she have been spooked by another spirit walking these halls?"

Amon rolled his eyes. Yes. Technically, he had once scared a woman while she was going down the stairs. That was very early on in his imprisonment and he hadn't expected her to get so scared she'd lose her footing. And all he did was bang on the door upstairs.

Most importantly, she didn't die. Amon noticed her falling and rushed down to catch her. Going corporeal for just that moment scared her enough to cause the couple to move. It kept him energized for a month, but she didn't *die.*

He waited for Neil to finish his speech and watched as they used some kind of device that flipped through radio channels. Amon couldn't be certain it wouldn't work if there was a ghost. But there wasn't and to him, it was just a loud, obnoxious noise.

He wanted to smack it from their hands, but he refused to give them any content. Then, they all freaked out when they saw...something? Amon was standing on the opposite side of the room, so it certainly wasn't him.

Once they finally finished, Amon jumped into action. He moved to the opposite side of the basement, made his hand solid, and pushed over a stack of empty paint cans.

The men gasped and Amon could taste their fear in the air. It wasn't sweet like Tana's, but it would do. He returned to full intangible form and moved back to the guys.

"What the fuck was that?" Kyle asked.

"Dude, get the camera," Neil said, making his way toward the sound. He wasn't scared like the others, but Amon planned on changing that.

Neil was ahead of the others, running over to get ready for whatever was going on. Amon waited until he got far enough away from the others, stood directly in front of Neil, and became solid.

Neil crashed right into him. He backed up, confused at

first, until he met Amon's eyes. Amon could see the red light of his eyes reflecting across Neil's horrified face. He'd used his magic to make himself appear even bigger than normal. Amon almost never used this much magic, and it felt good. Almost like stretching a muscle after being still for a long time.

Neil screamed like a child, and as much as Amon wanted to laugh, he schooled his features. Once the other men came he shifted and moved to the back.

"You okay?" Josh asked when they approached.

"I'm fine," Neil snapped, shoving the other man away. When the others got close, and he noticed one of them recording, he used his magic to throw the camera across the room.

"What the hell?" Kyle yelled.

He picked up the camera, and they all bolted upstairs. Amon laughed for a moment then quickly went back to Tana. She was still sleeping peacefully. He laid beside her, feeling his revenge had been a success.

With any luck, the ghost hunters would soon be running scared...and then he would have Tana all to himself.

12

TANA

"Tana," Kay called as she knocked on Tana's door.

Her tone spoke to trouble. Tana groaned, turning to where Amon used to be, finding him gone. She sat up, worried that last night was just some hookup to him. Of course it was. What else would it have been? Just because she thought there were feelings, doesn't mean there actually were.

Before her thoughts could spiral any further, she saw a note sitting on her side table. It was written in a surprisingly tidy hand, in looping, almost archaic cursive.

Went to shower, didn't want to wake you. See you later :).

She let her worry dissolve. He wouldn't be hitting and quitting and leave a note.

Right?

Kay knocked again, pulling Tana out of her memories of last night. She quickly threw on a robe and answered the door.

"Hey. Sorry to bother you. I know you've been really busy and had a lot on your plate, well I mean I guess we all kinda have -"

"Kay," Tana said, snapping her out of her babbling. "What is it?"

Kay paled. "Neil wants to see you."

"Did he say what about?"

"No, he wouldn't say. But he seemed pretty upset."

"Perfect." Tana followed Kay through the dining room toward the lobby.

Neil looked unhinged, with his rumpled hair and clothing, and wide eyes. She'd never seen him this disheveled. His crew didn't look much better, but equally confused.

As soon as Neil spotted her, he marched forward. "We need to leave. Right now."

Tana blinked, unsure what to say. "Well, all the roads are blocked right now so, -"

"Yes, I know that," Neil said. "I've called every cab company in a 30-mile radius and they've all said there's no way to get up here. But we need to go. You need to figure it out."

Tana was getting really sick of this guy. "And what would you like me to do about that, Mr. Cander?"

"What?"

"What would you like me to do?" she parroted, keeping her tone even. "I can't even move my own car. If no cab will come to get you, what do you want me to do about that?"

"I don't care!" Neil yelled, causing her to take a step back. "I don't care how you get us out of here, but you have to."

"Leaving so soon, Neil?" Amon said. Tana turned to see him standing behind her. Had he been there long? She hadn't even noticed him. "What's the rush? I thought you wanted to record more. Have you found anything yet?"

"Fuck off, dude. I'm not talking to you."

"Mr. Cander," Tana said, raising her hand, "please don't harass the other guests. I will call the plow company and see what's going on. They have yet to call me, but with the snow still coming down, I can't promise good news."

"Just get me out of here, or there will be hell to pay." He stalked off, his crew following silently.

"Well, he's truly a delight," Amon commented.

Tana sighed. She was more professional than to talk about one guest to another, but oh had she wanted to.

TANA SPOKE to the plow guy later that day and luckily, since the snow slowed, they were going to make it up the road. When she went to Neil's door to tell him as much, he told her to inform him when the plow was done and slammed the door. Even though he was still being unpleasant, at least he was no longer flirting.

When the plow finally came up the drive, a cab followed and Neil and his crew stalked out without a word.

Tana was relieved to see them gone. After they left, the bell above the door tinged and she looked up to see Bea.

"Hey girl, this is a surprise," Tana said, rounding the desk.

Bea looked worried, but instantly relaxed when she saw Tana. She ran to hug her like they hadn't seen each other in months. "Oh Tan, I'm so glad you're okay."

"Of course I am. We were just snowed in. You know Alise keeps enough food up here to feed a small army."

"No, not that. I was worried that -," she stopped mid-sentence and blinked at me, sniffing the air.

"What's going on, Bea? You're scaring me." Before she got to answer, Amon came down the stairs and stopped when he saw Bea.

"What are you doing here?" Bea asked in an accusatory voice.

Amon stood frozen by the stairs, as if unable to move.

"Do you know each other?" Tana asked.

"No," they said at the same time.

"We need to talk," Bea said. "You too," she pointed at Amon.

This did not seem good.

They all walked to Tana's room in silence. Tana's mind was reeling. What was going on? Bea and Amon said they didn't know each other, but that didn't seem true.

Were they together? Memories from before came flooding back and she wanted to run. But she needed to know, so she followed.

Once the door was shut, Bea wasted no time. "What the hell are you doing here?" she asked Amon again.

"I- I live here," he said.

"What?" Tana asked. "What do you mean you live here?"

"Why?" Bea asked, ignoring Tana completely. "I thought your kind loved traipsing around, causing chaos."

Your kind? Tana was trying to wrap her head around this conversation, but had no clue what was going on.

"I was summoned and hexed here. I've been here for a long time." Amon responded, looking at his joined hands.

"Impossible. I would have noticed by now." Bea accused once again.

"I've never seen you here till the other night," Amon said, voice rising. "And how did you find me anyway?"

"And why does she smell of you? What did you do to her?" Bea continued, ignoring his question.

"That isn't any of your business," he retorted.

"Alright!" Tana yelled. Her volume made them both stop

and remember she was still standing there. "What the fuck is going on?"

They both went silent, staring at each other. "Tell me. *Now*."

"Fine," Bea said. "But I need you to keep an open mind."

Tana nodded, perching on the edge of the hope chest at the foot of her bed. She was prepared for the worst.

"I'm a witch," Bea said.

That...had not been on the list of horrible possibilities.

Tana stared for a second, already more than a little annoyed. "Ha-ha, Bea. Stop messing around."

"She's not," Amon added, looking just as serious.

"Witches aren't real," Tana said in disbelief.

"Well, lore has to come from somewhere. And no way humans are that creative," Bea said with a hint of amusement in her voice. "But yes, it's true. I come from a long line of witches that have lived here for centuries. My Nan's apothecary is actually a magic supply shop. Aelmere Heights is kind of a...hub for paranormal beings."

Tana blinked. Neither Bea nor Amon looked like they were joking, but this seemed impossible. She compartmentalized what this meant and gestured for Bea to continue.

"Last week when I picked you up, I noticed a large amount of energy on the porch. I had heard this place was haunted, but ghosts barely leave a trace, so I knew it wasn't that."

"Wait, ghosts are real?" Tana asked.

"Yes, but that's not the point. I thought it was weird, so I slipped a power tracker into your purse."

"A what?"

"Not important," Bea said, continuing like everything was fine. "I felt a wild surge of energy and worried something happened to you. I booked it up here as soon as the roads cleared and now I find you smelling like a demon."

"Like a *what*?" Tana turned to Amon, waiting for an explanation.

Amon stuttered. "I—I'm what humans consider a demon. I was summoned by a witch a very long time ago. She hexed me because I refused to help her. I've been here ever since. Or that's the short of it anyway."

Tana closed her eyes and took a deep breath, trying to fit all this information in her head. "So wait, have you been haunting the inn? Are you the ghost?"

"I am not a *ghost*," Amon spit, as if she'd cursed at him. An involuntary giggle rose from her lips. Tana was pretty sure she was having a breakdown.

"But how? Everyone would see you."

One moment Amon was standing there, the next he was gone. Tana gasped. She stuck her hand out but nothing was there. When she brought her hand back he reappeared. "Holy shit!"

"Yes, yes, cool party trick," Bea said. Amon growled at the insult. "I want to know why you imprinted on her."

"Imprinted?" they said at the same time.

"Yes, she's obviously you're Fated. And you've left your mark on her. Anyone within a five-mile radius can smell a claim that strong."

Tana stared wide-eyed at Amon. What had he done to her? To his credit, he looked equally shocked.

"I didn't know," Amon said, meeting Tana's eyes. "I mean, she smelled different, and her fear tasted divine, but I didn't know what it meant. I have been here for many years and have never met anyone who met their Fated one before."

Bea peered at the two of them like she was trying to find

the truth. Tana wanted to ask what he meant by the taste of her fear, but she *definitely* wasn't prepared for the answer.

"Fine," Bea said after a minute. "I will help you."

"What?" Amon's eyes widened.

"I'm a witch, and you're Fated to my friend. You also don't seem to have that natural inclination for chaos and destruction like most demons. I'll speak to my Nan and see what she says."

"T-thank you," he said.

Bea nodded at him and then turned her attention to her friend. "Tan, I know this is a lot. But the world is the same, you just now have more knowledge of it."

Tana didn't know what to say, so she nodded.

"And with that, I'm going to go work on this and leave you two to discuss this whole...fated thing," Bea said. "Good luck!"

Bea turned and left, then, leaving Tana alone with Amon. Who was a...demon?

"So you're..." Tana said, trailing off.

"Yes."

"And we're..."

"Apparently."

They continued to stare at each other, neither of them sure of what to do.

"I think I need time to process all of this," Tana said finally.

Amon nodded in understanding. It seemed he needed time too. With that, he disappeared and Tana was left wondering what the hell to do now.

13

AMON

Damned witch, Amon thought as he sat in his room the next day.

Fated.

That was the word played over and over again since the day before. He never expected to meet his. He'd been trapped here so long, he never thought he'd meet anyone. Much less his Fated one. Not to mention a witch who may free him.

In the early days, he would constantly try to escape to no avail. No amount of magic or force he had would allow him off the property. After a while, he gave up and found other ways of keeping busy–most of which involved scaring others.

And even though he still cursed that witch for exposing him, he still felt a small glimmer of hope. Previous experience told him to be wary of witches, but this one seemed different. After all these years, he may have found a way out, a lifeline. And he didn't see how his situation could get any worse.

A light tap on the door had him springing to his feet and

swinging the door open. Tana stood on the other side. Her hair was in two braids that started from the top of her head and had on a knit sweater and leggings. She was so beautiful, Amon wasn't sure how he'd not seen she was his fated one.

"May I come in?" she asked.

"Of course." He moved over, allowing her to enter. She walked around the space, looking everywhere but at him. Amon couldn't blame her; yesterday was a lot, and he *knew* demons existed.

"So. You're not human," she said. Not a question like it was yesterday, but a statement. A fact.

"No." He watched her, gauging her reaction. She was still calm, which seemed like a good sign.

"So, this isn't what you look like?"

"No. It's an illusion."

"I would like to see what you look like."

That made Amon pause. "What?"

"I want to know what you actually look like. No illusion."

He wanted to refuse. What if she rejected him? But she deserved the truth. After a minute of further thought, he nodded.

He closed his eyes, afraid to see her reaction, and released the spell holding his illusion. After a few seconds, and no taste of fear, he opened his eyes. He had expected a look of shock or horror, but she looked more thoughtful.

Assessing.

"You're taller," she observed after what felt like a millennia.

A laugh bubbled from his chest. "Yes. Most humans aren't seven feet tall."

"They also tend not to be red," she said with a laugh. Relief flooded Amon when he realized she wasn't afraid or horrified. That was something at least. He could feel his tail swing back and forth behind him.

"You have a tail?" she gasped and walked around to get a better view. "Can I touch it?"

"I would prefer not," he said quickly as she reached forward.

She snapped her hand back. "Oh, sorry."

"No, it's okay. It's just, um, sensitive."

"Oh," she replied, cheeks reddening. "Well anyway. I wanted to see. I had to know. I'm not sure about this whole fated thing, but now I know you're not a...giant spider or anything, I feel much better."

"Spider?" he questions.

"Well. I didn't know. I've never seen a demon. Anyway, I'm heading out to meet Bea. She said her Nan wanted to talk to me. When I come back, I'd like to talk."

"I'd like that too," he said honestly.

She smiled and nodded at him before she left. A sense of relief washed over him. Amon grabbed his book once again. He worried about what they were talking about without him, but it wasn't like he could follow. He could only hope they would help him.

14

TANA

Tana got in her car and headed to Cabot Apothecary to meet up with Bea and her Nan. Bea's text was a bit ominous, which made her nervous.

When she arrived she quickly went inside, eager to get out of the cold. Even though the snow finally stopped, the chilled air was still harsh.

Bea stood at the counter arranging some sort of product. The shop was one of many along a street of miscellaneous vintage stores and bookshops. Tana thought about how many could be housing magic or other beings she had always been blissfully unaware of.

Cabot Apothecary was small with dark wood counters and shelves. The walls were covered with products meant to heal different ailments, and magical ingredients she supposed.

"Hey Tan," Bea said when she noticed Tana.

"Hey." It was silly, but now that she knew Bea could do magic, and Tana could barely boil water, she felt awkward and even...lesser. She quickly pushed those thoughts away. Bea had been nothing but kind since they met. She'd held Tana's hair after one too many drinks and still wore that hat with uneven edges Tana made her when she was learning to crochet. Bea never treated Tana any differently so Tana shouldn't either.

"Nan," Bea called into the back, "Tan's here."

"I'm comin', I'm comin'," a voice called from the back. Bea's Nan was a short woman, with dark skin and wrinkles lining her otherwise regal face. She had long, gray locks that were styled half-up half-down. She wore a long flowing tunic dress that made her look like the witch she apparently was.

"This is the one that is fated to the demon?" she asked in an accusatory fashion.

"Nan," Bea scolded.

She waved Bea off and continued to leer. Tana felt a bit scrutinized under her gaze, but refused to let it show.

"Follow me," she finally said, "Beatrix, throw up the closed sign and join us."

In the back, there was a small table with some chairs she led them to. It looked like a small kitchen but was obviously used for brewing as opposed to cooking. There were no giant cauldrons or tongue of newt lying around, but the various powders and empty jars signaled it wasn't meant for food.

"Would you like some tea, dearie?" Nan asked.

"Please," Tana said. Bea came back and produced a kettle of boiling water and a tea bag. Tana's hands itched to help, but she resisted, not wanting to be in the way. The ceramic cups clinked as Bea finished and settled in.

Once everyone was there, Nan turned to Tana. "So, start from the beginning."

Tana eyed Bea, making sure it was fine, then went through recounting everything that had happened. The haunted inn, the snow, Amon. She even vented about Neil and how awful he was.

When Tana was finished, Nan looked deep in thought. "And this demon, Amon, he's never caused harm?"

"Not that I can tell," Tana said. "I mean, there are stories about the inn. But I did extensive research when I was still curious about the legitimacy of the hauntings, and I don't think anyone's ever died on the property."

"Hm. Okay. I will break his hex. It will take a few days to gather the necessary supplies. I will come to the inn in four days when the full moon comes."

"Thank you," she said, shoulders sagged in relief. Even if she wasn't sure about Amon and this fated stuff, she didn't believe he deserved to be trapped anymore.

Nan disappeared up the stairs, and Bea walked Tana to the front of the store.

"This is all so crazy," Tana said to Bea once they were alone.

"I know," she said in an understanding tone. "But look at it this way, now we have no secrets."

Tana huffed a laugh. "Can I ask you a question?"

"Anything."

"What does being fated mean? I know I should be asking Amon this, but what if everything he says is because of this strange bond between us? Does anyone get a say in the matter? I don't want to be connected to him just because some all-powerful force crammed us together and said figure it out."

Bea smirked at her, letting her finish her rambling. "Being fated means you are a perfect match. You are meant to be together because you fit. Technically, it's an evolutionary trait in most paranormal species. When you've lived as long as most of us, normal human emotions are erased. Priorities change. We tend to be untrusting of others, relying heavily on instinct. Because of this, many didn't mate, and in turn, the population of many species went down. To us, it's just another sense. But many never find their fated. It's considered a gift."

"But what if I don't like him? Or he doesn't like me?"

"These bonds can always be broken, but very few choose to. Most who do believe the bond makes them weak, and would prefer a life full of loneliness over having any type of vulnerability. Those are typically ancient beings who have lost what you would consider humanity long ago."

Tana tried to wrap her head around all this. "Does that mean if everything works out and I fall for him, he can't love me?"

"That's not what I mean," Bea replied. "It's more like... many of us have seen a lot. It's hard to have the same feelings when you've lived for hundreds of years. Just talk to him."

Tana was trying to wrap her head around this. "Thanks, Bea."

"Of course. Just consider me your personal tour guide to all things paranormal."

Tana was about to leave when she thought of something. "Wait. How old are you?"

Bea smiled. "A lady never tells."

TANA KEPT HERSELF BUSY, excusing herself to do errands around town. Since the inn was open again and the staff could come back, she was able to sneak out. Kay, Lawerence, and Alise were given the day off as well; though Alise's husband had to all but drag her from the kitchen now that there were guests to feed.

Tana walked around town, mostly window shopping at small stores. She had already gone to her favorite craft store and spent way too much money on yarn.

In her travels, Tana found herself in Emery's Bookshop. It was a small shop with lots of exposed brick and local art. Books were piled high throughout the space. Some on shelves and tables, others in large stacks on the floor.

A man who she assumed to be Mr. Emery sat at the front of the store, reading a book of his own. Tana perused the shelves for a while, enjoying the cozy atmosphere and smell of books. The quiet gave her time to think, which she desperately needed, but was also sick of.

She'd spent the entire previous day thinking about what all this means. Ghosts are real. Witches are real. Demons are real. And she sorta had sex with one. It was a lot to wrap her head around.

And then there was this whole fated thing. She couldn't stop thinking this was a primal instinct driving him to her as opposed to any actual feelings. Even she couldn't deny the strange electricity between them. But was that her, or some base instinct she had?

As she contemplated all of these things she came across a book that piqued her interest. *Dating Satan: a Demonic Romance Novel.* A laugh bubbled from her lips. This felt like another twisted joke by fate herself.

Fine.

If fate wasn't going to quit, she wouldn't either. She walked right up to the register and bought the book. Mr.

Emery gave her a strange look for her reading choice, but she could care less. Tana wondered what he would think if he knew how close this was to her reality.

She left the bookstore and headed toward the inn, finally ready to talk to Amon.

15

TANA

"You know, that book is awful," Tana said, standing in front of Amon. When she came in he was in the reading nook, lost in a book.

"I quite like this one," he said with a smile. "I've actually read it before." She laughed, now feeling more unsure than she had earlier in the bookstore.

"Can we talk?" she asked.

He nodded. She grabbed his hand, and he followed, leaving the book on the chair. She paused at the door, making sure there was no one at the desk and continued to the stairs.

When they got to her room, she shut and locked the door. Tana turned to him. His eyes held flecks of passion that stole her breath. That couldn't be just instinct, right?

He was back in his human form, and now that she'd seen his true form, this didn't seem right.

"I want to talk to *you,*" she said.

His face flickered with concern, but he still shifted. Just like last time, his skin was bright red. He grew to at least seven feet tall not including the medium-length horns that jutted from his hair. They were curved slightly and tipped at the top. His eyes were still black now matching his hair, which was previously red.

She thought it was interesting that his skin color became his hair color while he was human as if he couldn't hide everything. And the tail! It was long enough to drag on the floor if he let it, and it had a heart-shaped, flat tip.

When she went to him earlier, she wanted to know if she even found him attractive. If she didn't, she didn't even want to consider continuing down this path. It was vain, but she had no clue what to expect. But even with the red skin and horns she couldn't deny how attractive he was.

They sat on the edge of her bed. Binx took that moment to rub against Amon's leg. She really liked that giant red guy. Tana was careful not to touch him, but couldn't help the smile that came to her lips when she heard his tail flapping against the fabric.

"Sorry," he said shyly, grabbing his tail. "It's got a mind of its own."

"It's fine," she giggled. After that, they sat in silence for a few moments. What was anyone supposed to say now? "Can you tell me how you got here?" she asked.

"It was a long time ago," he said, looking thoughtful. "My kind doesn't have any religious affiliation, but humans regarded us as devils and connected the two I suppose. I was summoned by a witch who lived here at the time. Sometimes, witches summon us to trap us. A lot of my kind liked to cause chaos and witches would try to stop us. But this witch wanted me to help her destroy the town and whatever else she had in mind. Essentially act as a pet. People think that if they summon a demon, they're obligated to obey, which isn't true. I'm not a genie."

"Are those real?" Tana interrupted, unable to help herself.

"Genies? Maybe. I've never seen one but who knows? Some creatures have basically never been seen. I've only seen a dragon once. They tend to stick to their caves."

"There are dragons?!"

"Yes, snow bunny, there are dragons. Anyway...this witch got angry and cast a trapping spell on me. She thought if I was stuck here, I would do what she wanted just to escape, but I still refused. After a few years, she left and sold the place, leaving me here."

Tana's chest was constricted by his words. He'd been kept here against his will for all this time. Not that they were comparable, but she felt like she could relate a little. "And earlier... you said something about eating fear."

"Ah. Yes. My kind eats, it's just emotions we eat as opposed to food. I'm sure you've heard of a succubus. They are just demons who eat lust. I consume fear."

"And that's why you scare the guests?"

"Partly. I mean, let's be honest, people experience enough fear that I probably wouldn't need to. But if you've been here as long as I have, you get bored."

"So. How old are you then?"

He looked thoughtful again. "Three-hundred and ten give or take a few years."

Tana sputtered, shock evident on her face. "Holy shit."

"I'm quite young for my kind." She stared at him, mouth agape. "I'm serious. We live seven hundred years, give or take." That didn't help at all.

Tana's mind was spiraling. If he was hexed here so long ago, he'd have spent most of his life here. "What about your parents?"

"My parents passed away a long time ago. There was a

war when I was a youngling. My kind tends to be very territorial and greedy. One clan was inching into another's territory and it caused many battles. My parents were lost, and I...left. Unlike the rest of my kind, I was not territorial and did not care for war."

Tana's heart twisted once again.

"I'm sorry." She knew that wasn't enough, but there were no words that would ever be enough.

"It was a long time ago."

"Were your parents Fated?"

"No. Most don't find their Fated. It is rare amongst my kind. Any kind for that matter. Most decide to find a mate in a more traditional fashion."

"But what if they mate with someone, and then find their Fated?"

"Most choose their Fated." He said, causing Tana to suck in loudly.

"It may seem harsh," he continued, "but they are considered your perfect match, handpicked by the goddesses. Most do not wish to go against that."

Tana took it all in. So if he had found someone, and then found me, would he have abandoned them? Would he abandon her?

"Tana," he said, pulling her from her thoughts. "Talk to me."

"This is just a lot," she said honestly, looking at the ground. "I mean, I talked to Bea and did a lot of thinking, but I can't help thinking that we don't get to choose to be together. That it's just written in the stars and we have no choice in the matter."

He grabbed her hand and she looked at him. "I don't want you to ever feel like you don't have a choice. Yes, some people choose each other because they believe that is the will of the goddess, and choosing anything else is wrong. I've heard of Fated ones being miserable together, but staying because they were Fated."

Her gaze fell away. "However," he said, lifting her chin to meet his eyes, "I do not believe such things. Realistically, fate has a hand in everything. I believe that the fates put us together, and I believe we are meant for each other. But I don't believe anyone should force themselves to stay just because they are fated. I just want to take it day by day. Learn about each other. I want us together because we chose us."

She had to blink back the pressure she felt behind her eyes, refusing to let tears cloud this moment.

"I want that too." He smiled at her words and she smiled back warmth spreading in her chest. She leaned in and he met her halfway, slanting his lips over hers. He deepened the kiss, pushing his tongue into her mouth.

"Want to go to bed?" she asked when she pulled away to breathe.

"I would like nothing more."

16

AMON

Before Tana could stand, Amon swept her off her feet. She squealed as he carried her to the bed at a somewhat inhuman speed. Binx was on the bed and quickly left in a huff, annoyed that her sleep was disturbed.

He laid her down and removed her clothes as fast as possible. Once she was naked in front of him, he took his fill of her.

Her deep brown curls lay messily across the pillows. She was soft everywhere and had thighs he wanted to take a bite out of. And he couldn't even think about her round ass that bounced with every step. It was enough to drive him mad.

She reached for his cock and he flinched. She snapped her hand away, but he grabbed it.

"Sorry," he said. "It's just a bit...different than you may be used to." The look on her face made it clear that made him more intriguing. He leaned in, inhaling her addicting scent. "My naughty little snow bunny," he murmured into her hair.

Amon adjusted so he could take his pants off so she

could see. He had a thick mushroom tip with a ribbed shaft and a sizable knot at the bottom.

Her eyes widened in fascination. "I—I don't think that's gonna work," she said.

"Don't worry bunny. It will fit." He lay on the bed and placed her on top of him. He slid his tail up between her legs, letting the thick tip massage her clit. She cried out, grinding down on him, trying for more friction. He didn't give her any, however, backing off when she pressed down.

She whined in protest, but he was having none of that. He removed his tail fully and smacked the end against her ass. Tana hissed through her teeth. He did it again on the other side and she moaned this time. She ground down again, looking for friction.

"Oh, my snow bunny like's a little pain, doesn't she?"

"Yes," she ground out as he smacked her again. He flicked her nipple and she leaned into the sensation.

Amon shifted them so he was in the middle of the bed with her hips hovering right above his face. He pulled her down against her face and feasted as if he was a starving man.

Using his tongue, he pushed into her folds, pleasantly surprised by how wet she already was for him. She fought to keep her weight off him but he wanted to be crushed between those delicious thighs.

"Amon," she moaned. His name on her tongue made him want to come instantly.

He doubled his efforts, tugging and sucking on her clit, adjusting based on her reaction. He leaned her forward slightly and tipped his hips so he could force his tail between them and pushed it into her.

Amon growled at the sensation and she gasped. He

reached up with one hand to play with her nipples again, sending her closer to the edge.

"Yes, come for me bunny." At that, she tightened around his tail and moaned loudly. She rode out her climax, grinding against him. Wetness filled his mouth and he reveled in the taste. He didn't think he'd ever get enough.

When she finally finished, she made her way down his body. He tried to catch her, since they were far from done, but stopped once he realized where she was going. She wasted no time, taking him right into the warm heat of her mouth.

"Fuck," he growled.

She licked and sucked every inch of him and it took all his strength not to come. She took him deep in her mouth, down her throat. When she swallowed around him he swore he saw stars.

He quickly hauled her up, refusing to come anywhere but that sweet pussy. He positioned her over him. She grabbed him to line him up and started sinking down.

He bit his lip so hard he tasted blood. She was tighter than he could have imagined. Tana worked herself up and down, getting further each time. He squeezed her thighs, guiding her further down.

After a few more thrusts she fit everything but the knot. She leaned down so their faces were hovering over each other.

"You feel so fucking good," he told her, running his fingers through her hair. The kiss was slow and heavy. "Let me know when you want to move," he murmured into her lips.

She nodded almost imperceptibly and wiggled experimentally. It took a lot to not come on the spot. He took a deep breath, fighting the instinct to thrust without abandon.

"I'm ready," she said breathlessly. He didn't need to be told twice. He pulled out almost fully and thrust back into her. She matched his rhythm thrust for thrust and he became lost in the feeling of her tight, slick heat.

"Oh gods," she cried.

"No gods here. Just a little bunny and her demon." Reaching between them he rubbed her clit once more. He let her set the pace, let her chase her release.

Bringing his tail up, he gave her one more smack before she exploded, crying his name. She rode out her climax, flooding him once again.

Amon quickly flipped them, boxing her in between his hands. "I wanna knot you bunny. Can I?"

"Yes," she breathed, wrapping her hands around his neck and bringing him in for a kiss. He slowly pressed, working it into her. After a few thrusts, he worked it in.

There was no way to last now, but he wanted her to come one more time. He used his fingers to play with her clit and tilted back, changing the angle.

"Right there," she cried.

"Come for me bunny, I need it." She chased her pleasure and soon he felt the telling squeeze. His balls drew up and with one final thrust, he shot his load deep inside.

"Fuck." Amon released untill he was sure the only thing keeping it all in was his knot. In his three hundred-some-odd years he'd never come that hard. He rolled them so they were side to side and pulled her close.

"Are we stuck?" she said, testing with a wiggle.

Amon hissed. "Yes. And we'll be stuck together forever if you keep doing that." He could feel himself harden again.

"Really," she said, drawing the syllables out. She wiggled again, the sensation sending shivers up his spine.

He moaned. "Who knew my adorable snow bunny was a minx in disguise."

She giggled and pulled him into a kiss.

"Round two?"

17

TANA

After another round and a bit more teasing, Amon's knot went down and Tana was able to slip out. When she did, cum flooded from her and she ran to the bathroom. Amon said he was going to change the sheets while she took a bath. She insisted he didn't need to, but he was adamant. Tana told him where to find the sheets and slipped into the bath.

She thought about things with Amon, their talk. His words were so sincere she felt no reason to doubt him anymore. They would take it one day at a time.

She finished her bath and threw on an oversized crew neck sweater and some panties.

She had to be sorta classy.

When she stepped into the bedroom, the lights were off and the fireplace was burning brightly. The bed was made and there was Amon.

He sat on what looked like a nest of pillows and blankets, no doubt from the linen closet.

She rushed over and cuddled up with him. Binx laid on her own pillow beside them. Leaning forward, she reached for her drink and curled back up into Amon's side. He put one arm around her and wrapped his tail around her, resting it on her shoulder. Tana didn't think anything could match this moment of total bliss.

"Did I finally convert you to the mint chocolaty side?" she asked Amon, watching him take a large sip.

"No. This is black coffee," he said.

She scrunched her nose. "That's gross."

"Is not."

"What is good about bitter bean juice?"

"What's good about chocolate-y toothpaste?"

She gave an indignant gasp. "You take that back."

"Never."

They talked for a while after that. He told stories of the people who'd lived there before it was an inn and different guests he'd scared out the door. She told him about the day she got Binx and leaving her parents. She even told him about Courtney.

"Ah. Is that why you were going though my stuff that day."

Tana gasped again. "Was not."

"You definitely were." Amon said. "But it's okay. I wasn't mad then, and I'm not mad now."

Tana relaxed once more into him, glad he didn't mind her snooping.

"Oh my god," she gasped suddenly.

"What?" he asked. Concern growing on his features.

"We didn't use a condom. Am I going to get pregnant? Are we even compatible in that way? I don't think I'm ready for a baby." Her thoughts tumbled out of her mouth at a rapid pace.

"Tana, it's okay," Amon said soothingly. "Yes, we are

compatible. All fated are. However, Bea should be able to make you some sort of birth control spell. Just ask her."

"And you're okay with that?"

He thought for a moment. "I would like younglings one day. However, I want one when we are both ready." She sighed a breath of relief, relaxing into him once more. They hunkered down on the couch and continued talking once more.

"MOM, THE ROADS JUST CLEARED," Tana said for what felt like the millionth time. She had been avoiding her mother's calls for a few days but, ever persistent, she called three other times that day and Tana knew she would have to face her, eventually.

"So why aren't you in your car on the way home? Christmas is in three days."

"I know. I just had a lot going on and now that we're open again we're booked up." That was a lie. While they did have quite a few guests, Tana probably could have left. And while deep down she felt guilty about avoiding them, the idea of going home after everything else felt wrong. She wanted to be here when Amon was set free.

"Tana, you could be doing much more than running some mom-and-pop inn. Just come home, forget about that job. Your father and I have a big surprise for you this year."

She didn't even want to know what it was. "I will try. But I might not be able to come till after Christmas. I promise to still come, it just might be late."

"Fine. Choose that crappy job over your family." With that, her mother hung up on her.

Tana sighed. Her mom tried to guilt trip her with that constantly, and while it didn't have the same impact as it used to, it still hurt.

Tana walked back to her room, ready to be done with the day. Amon cornered her as soon as she got to her room.

"Hi bunny, I want to show you something." While she wasn't really in the mood, seeing his face light up made her melt.

"No more snow bunny?" she asked. She initially wasn't a fan of that nickname, but it soon became endearing.

"Well, that's implied; it won't snow forever. Maybe I can change it to hopper."

She rolled her eyes and shoved him.

He laughed and she followed him down the hall. He was in his human form and while it had initially been a shock to see him as not human; she was starting to prefer his natural version much more. They walked until they hit 5E. He gestured for her to unlock it and she used her master key to open the door. Luckily none of the guests were staying there now. They walked to the wall on the far side and he stopped in front of it.

Tana stared at him like he'd grown a second head. "So you wanted to show me...a wall?"

"Just wait," he said impatiently. She wasn't sure how exciting this wall could possibly be until he turned incorporeal and disappeared.

She was not a fan of this particular skill.

A few moments later, she heard movement and the wall broke. Tana thought he brought her here so she could watch him destroy a wall. She was about to tear him a new one when she noticed it was a door behind the wallpapered wall, he had just opened it.

She stepped through carefully and was quite surprised by what she found.

There was so much...stuff.

Piles of books, full jewelry boxes, and even some furniture.

"What is this?" She asked.

"I guess you could say it's my home," Amon said. "When I got trapped here, I started collecting things. This room used to be a bedroom and a sitting area. Eventually, my collection became pretty large, so when the place was between owners I walled off the sitting area and kept it for myself."

"How did no one notice there was a sitting room missing?"

"I used magic to compel them. Also, people tend to believe what they want so," he shrugged.

Tana moved around the space, taking in the large amounts of stuff. Silk tapestries hung from the walls and she noticed a pile of cat treats on a small table.

"Do you let Binx in here?" she asked.

Amon stuttered in protest, but never answered. She knew the big old demon had a soft spot for the little guy. She continued around the room, taking an interest in everything from the chests of jewelry to the very old-looking dresses and suits.

Tana looked at Amon, who was watching her like a predator. This was a common look from him, and she knew exactly what it meant. Her face heated under his hungry gaze, and his nostrils flared in response.

"I can smell you," he said, causing her face to heat even further.

"You can smell that?" she asked, feeling a bit exposed.

"I have a very good nose, bunny." He stepped closer.

Feeling giving after being shown this very private part of his life, Tana stalked forward, now feeling more predatory herself. Amon seemed to like the shift, dominance leaving his features. While this was a side Tana hadn't expected, she ate it up.

Tana pushed him up against an old, ornate vanity and he leaned back, following her lead. She was surprised it didn't break under his weight, but it held, only giving the slightest creak.

Tana launched forward, devouring his mouth. She'd never taken charge of their kiss before, but he gave in easily, allowing her to set the pace. Tana pulled back and all but ripped at his jeans, forcing them down. She sank to her knees and took him in almost to the hilt, swallowing deeply around him.

"*Fuuck,*" he moaned. He fisted her hair, not to take control, but as an anchor. She continued up and down at an agonizing pace. Every time she felt him nearing his end, she would let up, giving his balls a heavy squeeze.

"Bunny, you're going to kill me."

"Oh, my big bad demon can't handle it?" she chided.

He growled in response, eyes flaring red. She continued, pushing and pulling, giving and taking. Tana had never thought herself to be dominant. She never thought herself much of anything when it came to sex. She'd had a fair number of partners and whether male or female, it never lasted long enough to explore anything.

But with Amon, she felt this sense of rightness. Everything connected perfectly, and now there was no more faking pleasure or fighting for it. Now it was just there, like it was always supposed to be. And she was learning she liked giving and getting pleasure in equal measure.

She lifted off of him fully, and he whined. Her three-hundred-year-old demon boyfriend *whined*. Tana couldn't resist her laugh.

She dragged him to the floral couch across the room and plopped him down. He tapped his fingers on his thighs, obviously trying not to reach out for her. Tana slowly raised her shirt, watching his eyes roll over her pink lace bralette. Once the shirt was gone, she turned around, pushing her pants slowly down over her bottom and down her thighs, leaving only a small scrap of pink lace left. She had been planning to jump him when she got off work anyway, so she was happy she prepped. Bent over, Tana's eyes met Amon's heated gaze. She put her hands on the coffee table in front of her and leaned forward, exposing her even more.

"You coming?" she asked playfully. In less than a second Amon kneeled behind her, running his hands up and down her thighs. It felt like she was being worshiped. Amon worked her panties down slowly, and she could feel the cold air against her very wet pussy.

"Fuck, bunny," he said, "you're dripping wet." He pushed his finger through her folds, making her call out in pleasure. While there wasn't anyone in 5E right now, she still worried they would be heard by the other patrons. "The walls are soundproofed with magic, bunny, be loud for me."

That was all the motivation she needed. She cried out, loving the way he teased her. Amon closed in, licking her hard. Tana hadn't noticed how long his tongue was before, but he shoved the thick muscle deep, reaching that spot inside that made her insides twist with pleasure. He was relentless, lapping her up. When he pulled away, she expected him to retreat, but he instead aimed higher, dragging his tongue over her backside to her tight hole. She gasped, unfamiliar with the sensation.

Amon continued lapping her hole, and was soon loosening her and making his way inside. She'd never been comfortable enough to try this, but with Amon, she felt at ease. He snaked his tail up her thigh and pressed it against her clit, rubbing vigorously.

The dexterity he had with that thing was incredible.

Soon, he replaced his tongue with his finger, sliding it inside. She wasn't expecting it to be so slick until she turned back and saw a bottle of lube resting on the table. Tana didn't even want to know which guest he acquired that from. Soon one became two, and he was scissoring his fingers, stretching her out. Even though it was a new sensation, it wasn't an unpleasant one. And once he was working a third in, Tana was ready for something more. "Amon, please," she cried. Any more words than that would have been too much for her brain.

Amon pulled out fully, leaving her empty. "You ready, snow bunny?" he asked. She felt his hard cock lined up with her hole. She nodded, and he sank in slowly. Tana ground her teeth, feeling herself stretch around him. "Breath, bunny," he soothed. She took a deep breath, and soon, he pushed past that first tight ring and much of the pressure ceased. He took short thrusts, working himself deeper every time. Once he was fully seated, he paused, giving her time to relax.

She took some more breaths, wiggling experimentally around him. Amon moaned, and she loved this power she felt she held. The pleasure she gave him. "Ready, bunny?" he asked.

"Yes," she said, sounding more like a plea, and he slowly started moving. This was a totally new experience for her, but she loved it. His tail roamed around again, finding its way into her front, and she screamed in pleasure. She had never felt so full before. He growled behind her, right next to her ear. "You have no idea how good you feel," he moaned breathlessly. "I'm gonna fill this tight little ass up. But first I need you to come for me." His words were her undoing. Tana spiraled, allowing pleasure to overtake her. She could feel herself tightening around him, causing him to hiss. Heat filled her as he released, filling her as promised.

Amon carefully pulled out. He grabbed Tana and pulled her to a surprisingly large couch. She cuddled into his chest as he rubbed her back. They basked in the afterglow, content just to hear each other breathe.

"My mom called today," Tana said, breaking the silence. Amon growled. She'd told him what happened between them, why she left. "I want you to come with me. You know, when you're freed." He stilled and she could feel the tension in his body. "If you don't want to, it's fine," she continued. She worried he was uncomfortable with the idea. "I know meeting the parents can be scary, I just thought -,"

"Bunny," Amon said, cutting her off. "I would love to meet your parents. I'm just a bit... out of practice with socializing. I wouldn't want to embarrass you."

Her heart twinged at his words. "If anything, they will probably embarrass themselves. I know this isn't really selling the trip, but my parents will probably say things that sound outwardly nice but are actually backhanded the entire time. I don't want to put you in that situation, but I can't help but want you there."

Emotion flickered in his eyes. "Okay."

"Okay?"

"I'll come. But I can't promise to tolerate any bad talk about you."

"Deal," she said, cozying back up to him. For the first time in a long time, Tana was looking forward to going home.

18

AMON

The day seemed to drag on agonizingly slow. Amon waited in Tana's room, Binx cuddled up on his side. Even the soft hum of the purring cat wasn't enough to calm his nerves. It was the night before the full moon and he itched to be free. Even though he didn't plan on going very far, it would be nice to be able to go anywhere.

Tana finally returned around eight, looking gorgeous as ever. Whether this girl was in sweats or dressed up, she glowed.

"Bea's Nan is here," she said, crossing the room and petting Binx on the head. Amon knew it was foolish to be jealous of the little creature, but the attention she received made him crazy. Tana could see the look on his face and moved over to him, straddling his lap.

She patted the top of his head. "Is this better?"

He rolled his eyes, but inside he preened at the attention. Who knew a human would one day swoop in and cause him to bend at her will? If she asked him to destroy the world and remake it in her image, he would. The obsession ran way deeper than he was willing to admit to her yet.

However, even his mate in his lap wasn't enough to completely ignore the gnawing anxiety blooming inside of him. "Why?"

"She didn't say. She just wanted to talk to us both."

He tensed. Was freeing him impossible?

"It's all going to be okay," Tana said soothingly. Even without the full fate bond, she was so in tune with him. "Bea and her Nan are the best witches I know."

"They're the only ones you know, bunny," he pointed out. She shushed him and he laughed, lifting them both to their feet.

They walked together to the dining room. It was pretty late so no one was around. Bea's Nan stood in the center, assessing Amon carefully. This was something he was used to from other paranormal beings. Demons were known for creating chaos, always causing their next meal, regardless of the consequences. He'd never been the type for that. Humans were constantly in fear of things, which made it easy to passively feed. He hadn't started interacting with them until he was trapped here, and that was more about entertainment than anything.

"So, you are the demon Amon," Nan said.

"Yes," he said.

"Why should I free you? Did the witch trap you here because you were wreaking havoc on her town?"

"No," he said firmly. "I was halfway across the world in Mumbai when I was suddenly whisked here by Katerina." Nan's nose wrinkled at the name, so he assumed she must be familiar. "She summoned me to take over the town, but I refused. In anger, she hexed me here."

Nan nodded in understanding. "Very well. Yes, I knew

Katerina, and unfortunately, that's just the beginning of her long list of terrible deeds. Well. you'll be happy to know, I found a way to break the hex. It is a powerful one, mind you, and breaking it comes with a price." Amon awaited anxiously, wanting to know what he had to do.

"To clarify, you have been tied to this estate," Nan continued. "I cannot remove the anchor that has been placed on you, but I can tie it to something else using a different kind of connection." Nan eyed Tana.

Her eyes widened. "Me?"

"Yes. You are his Fated one, I can remove the anchor he has and link it to you. Since you are living, you won't be tied by proximity, but your souls will intertwine. Your lifetimes linked. When one of you goes, so does the other."

"Does that mean his life will shorten?" Tana asks.

"No, it means yours will lengthen. This is typical of Fated ones, to share extended lifetimes. But the draw you feel will be stronger. Spending long amounts of time apart will cause physical harm to both of you." Amon's heart sank. "I'll give you two time to think it over. I'll be back tomorrow night for your answer." And with that, she disappeared, leaving Amon and Tana there to make this giant decision.

19

TANA

Tana didn't know what to think. Her mind raced a thousand miles a minute trying to make sense of the solution Bea's Nan came up with. The thought of being tied together forever didn't give her as much pause as she knew it should, which made her more nervous.

She barely noticed when they arrived at her room. They plonked down on the couch, sending Binx scurrying away. They sat and stared at each other, neither one knowing what to say first.

Amon broke first. "I'll wait."

"What?" she asked.

"I don't want to rush things. As much as I want to be free, I want you more. And I want you to want me. Doing this would add hundreds of years to your life, and trap you with me forever. I understand wanting time to think it over. And if I have to stay here a little longer, so be it."

He was so calm, she knew he meant it. His words resonated with her, solidifying her decision. "I'll do it," she said. He started shaking his head, but she pushed on. "I understand the commitment this is. And I understand that this would tie us forever, but we just...fit. Even though I was skeptical of the fate bond, I know, deep down, we should be together. And pushing the timeline might not have been in the plan, but *we* are in the plan." He blinked at her, a million emotions crossing his face.

"You're sure?" he asked evenly, still trying not to allow his emotions to change her mind.

"Always." Amon leaned in and kissed her deeply. She followed his lead, allowing him to pull her to bed.

20

AMON

They walked hand in hand to the backyard, getting as far into the forest line as Amon could reach. He was well acquainted with the invisible barrier, an old nemesis. Bea and her Nan were there. Bea shuffled through a bag, pulling out different jars and bags, while Nan flipped through a book, stopping when she found her page. The full moon cast a glow over the space, coating the darkness in a thin veil of light.

Tana stood next to him, his brave bunny. He checked with her over and over throughout the day. She stayed firm, ignoring his logic. Finally, she yelled at him, explaining that it was her eternity, not his. He had balked at her and apologized. Their first fight had ended pretty easily in Amon's opinion.

"You're sure about this?" he heard Bea ask Tana quietly. "You don't need to rush."

"I'm sure," she insisted, patting her friend on the shoulder.

Bea nodded and went back to assist her Nan. Amon moved to Tana, taking both hands in his. He didn't ask her again, for fear of her wrath, but she still squeezed his hands in reassurance. He took a deep breath and Nan walked up to them, ready to start.

"When you give her the mating bite, we will perform the spell. I understand mating is normally a very personal thing, so as soon as we are done, we will be on our way."

They nodded and faced each other again. "I didn't know there would be biting," Tana whispered in an amused fashion. "Kinky. Will it hurt?"

"Minx," Amon chided, but a smile crinkled his face all the same. "It may at first, but it will be fast."

She nodded. "Keep your hands linked until I'm done," Nan said.

"Ready, bunny?" He asked.

"As ever."

He began the fated bond. "I Amon, demon of fear, ask you, Tana Kane, to accept me as your Fated one. To allow me to protect you, care for you, and respect you for all of the time we have on this plane of existence, and beyond."

"I accept," she responded. "And I, Tana Kane, ask you Amon, demon of fear, to accept me as your Fated one. To allow me to protect, care, and respect you as you do me, on this plane, and the next."

"I accept," Amon replied, chest heavy with emotion. She leaned to the side, giving him full access to her neck. He leaned in, taking in her scent, and bit.

She tasted divine. She hissed initially, but melted into him, sighing deeply. Amon felt the bond snap in place, their souls intertwining. He felt her rush of emotion, the love and adoration pouring over him. He could lightly hear Nan around them, chanting ancient words he barely recognized and couldn't care about.

Amon felt the moment he was released from Camden

Inn. The weight he normally felt dissipated and the invisible barrier was no more. He broke free from Tana, watching as the bond bite shifted into a permanent mark. Nan and Bea were gone, and it was just him and his snow bunny. His need burned through him. "Do you trust me?" he breathed into her hair.

"Yes," she whispered.

"If there's anything you don't like, say candy cane."

"Candy cane?" she questioned.

"Yes. Because I plan to chase you down. And I have so much planned for when I catch you."

Her eyes widened and her fear permeated the air, as did her arousal.

"'Now. Run, snow bunny.'"

21

TANA

Tana took off, running through the trees, knowing Amon was following close behind. She normally avoided these woods for fear of coyotes, but she knew Amon would never let anything happen to her.

When that bond snapped in place she felt it. The longing and love he felt overwhelmed her, as if the feeling was her own. She sent her own love back, knowing he could feel it. She felt her body change, and while she didn't know exactly *what* was different, something was.

She weaved through the trees, narrowly avoiding tripping on small sticks in the brush. Tana felt genuine fear. Felt like she was being hunted. And, in a way, she was. Amon was close by. Watching her, stalking her. She had no clue where he was but she was determined to get away.

The trees rustled behind her, causing her to veer left, zigzagging to get away. Amon appeared before her and she screamed, falling back. Gathering herself, she quickly got up and kept going, ignoring the scratch on her knee.

Tana found herself in a clearing that she didn't want to

be in. It was too exposed. As she paused to run back, Amon rushed her, taking her down and lowering her into the snow. She fought back with a half-hearted instinctual urge, not really wanting to get away, but he was too strong. "Oh, what do we have here? A scared little bunny."

Tana continued struggling, deliberately rubbing her body against him to encourage her demon to let loose with his possession. She wanted it. She feared letting go when he was in this state. The two conflicting emotions collided until both were true, and if he had tried to walk away, she may have pounced on him herself. Amon worked her pants down, and she moaned. Her coat was long and covered her from the snow and Amon was so warm it was like a furnace.

"I can taste your fear, bunny. It's almost as delicious as this," he worked his hand into her panties and through her folds. She cried out, but he ignored her, bending down to suck on her nipple. The sensations were overwhelming in the best way possible, her mind devoid of everything outside of this moment.

They could feel each other's pleasure adding to their own. Tana had never experienced anything like this. She reached for him, running her hands up and down his shaft. "Need...you," Amon brokenly groaned.

"Take me," she said breathlessly. That was the only encouragement he needed. He dove directly in, taking her in one deep thrust. She matched his rhythm. His tail played with her clit and he leaned in to give her bruising kisses. She sucked on his tongue and his whole body shuttered. He kissed down her neck. When he licked over her sensitive bond mark, she was done for, her orgasm barreling into her.

Amon worked his knot in and came hard, filling her

with warmth. They lay there, stuck together by his knot. Even in the chilled air, she was ablaze, and happier than she'd ever been.

22

TANA

A week had gone by since Amon was released. Tana took some time off work and they traveled around, just driving wherever they wanted. They got in her car and started going. Amon asked they avoid places with a high concentration of paranormals, given their aversion to demons, which was easy considering Aelmere Heights was the biggest one for miles.

They saw museums and went to small bookstores. Tana even let Amon drive on long stretches where there was open highway and few other cars. Even though he'd never done it, he picked it up quickly. Tana took that time to work on her rug. While cumbersome in the car, she was set on finishing it.

On Christmas, they spent the day in some cute town that seemed to love the holiday. There were lights on every post and most houses had decked out their yards with blowup snowmen and reindeer. There was also a giant tree in the center of the town and a Christmas festival going on. One of the women at the stalls told them their town was so small, it was like spending time with family. Plus, tourists ate it up.

Tana told Amon she felt like she was in one of those Hallmark movies. They started building a narrative about a baker and some out-of-town businesswoman falling in love while walking around. They ended the night sitting on Tana's finished rug watching fireworks.

It was the best Christmas Tana had ever had.

Unfortunately, after a week of mind-blowing hotel sex and new adventures, they landed at Tana's parents' home. It was just after New Years and they still insisted on them coming and visiting. Kaya had been more than willing to watch Binx while they were away, and Tana was sure that the cat was still living like a princess in their absence.

They pulled up to the gated driveway, which opened to reveal a sprawling mansion with acres of land. It was an older place with colonial pillars and blue coloring. They pulled to the front around the topiaries in the middle of the driveway.

"Last chance to escape," Tana said.

"I'm sure it will be fine," Amon stated confidently. He didn't know how vicious her parents could be, but she shrugged and got out anyway, damning them to this fate. When they rang the doorbell a maid answered, one Tana had never seen before. That was no surprise; her mother never kept people employed for long.

The woman took their coats and brought them to the sitting room. Tana could remember spending time meeting potential suitors here in high school–ones from respectable families that were 'perfect' for her.

Tana wondered what her mother would think about a three-hundred-year-old demon.

Said demon was in his human skin, dressed in a tailored suit he bought on the way. Apparently, he had some money put away before he was trapped and from the looks of it, it was no small amount. The day before they went shopping, he got his suit and she got a deep green silk dress with thin straps and draped fabric on the top. It hugged her figure perfectly. She balked at the price, but Amon paid it, not thinking twice.

"Tana," her mother said, standing from the couch as they entered. She looked the same as the last time they met.

There was truly nothing Botox couldn't do.

Her blonde hair was neatly pinned in a tight bun and she wore a black dress and tons of jewelry.

"Hi mom," she said, leaning in for a hug. "This is Amon."

Her mother looked him over, assessing his tailored suit, and seemed mildly pleased. She shook his hand which was a miracle on its own. "Pleasure."

The maid made everyone a drink, and Tana downed half of hers in one shot.

You had to in this house.

"Kim," mother said, gesturing to the maid, "can you go tell James our guests are here?" Kim nodded and swiftly left. "So, Amon, what do you do?"

Tana rolled her eyes. This was always the first question. "I'm between jobs at the moment," he answered. She was sure she heard one of her mother's teeth crack. He winked at Tana and she choked on her drink.

"That's... nice. Tana dear, how's the inn?"

"It's fine. As you know, we were snowed in for a few days, so there has been a lot to do, but I was able to take some time off to come here." Tana hadn't mentioned the trip they took the week before.

"Hello Tana," her dad said when he entered the room.

"Hey, dad," she said, standing to hug him. Her dad was a tall man, with thinning gray hair and a thick, well-groomed beard. As usual, he was in a silk suit that was probably the cost of half her yearly salary. He was one of those hedge fund managers who could never retire. He'd tried a few years back, but he only lasted a few months. When boredom set in, he went back. Her mother was glad he went back. Without his work, she had much fewer events to plan. But now that he was working again, she could go back to planning extravagant parties and dinners for his staff and clients.

"Hello, Mr. Kane. I'm Amon." Amon held his hand out and her father took it reluctantly.

"Nice to meet you," her father said. "I understand this relationship is new."

"I guess," Amon said.

"And what do you do?"

"He's between jobs," her mother answered for him.

"Well, that sounds...freeing." Tana bit her tongue, trying to keep her anger concealed. They'd just gotten there, and she didn't want to argue five minutes in.

"Yes. I made some good investments back in the day and I had some savings so I decided to take a vacation. I went to Camden Inn, met Tana, and I guess the rest is history." He squeezed Tana's hand. They'd decided that story was close enough to the truth.

Her father looked interested in that. "Oh, you invest. I happen to know a lot about that if you ever need some tips."

"I may take you up on that, sir," Amon said. Somehow, that seemed to soothe her dad.

Tana leaned into Amon. "Are you the parent whisperer or something?"

He winked back at her.

They had drinks and dinner, all unnaturally pleasant. Amon has read a lot of business journals because he and her dad talked circles around her. "Maybe some of your business savvy will rub off on Tana," her dad said during dessert. "She decided not to follow in my footsteps and attend Princeton. She decided on one of those online scams."

"Dad, just because I didn't go to Princeton, doesn't mean I don't know things. Or that my college isn't real. Also, neither of you even expected me to finish."

"We most certainly did," her father chimed in. "Just because we wanted you to meet someone, doesn't mean we didn't want you to be educated."

"He's just saying you didn't take a very conventional route," her mom chimed in. "But it still seems like you found yourself a good man. We thought we were going to have to set her up." She said to Amon, as if Tana wasn't sitting right there. "We'd actually invited some of our friends with single sons to come meet you at the holiday party."

"You did *what*?" Tana fumed.

"Well dear, you aren't young forever. We just want you to be taken care of."

Tana shared a knowing glance with Amon. Little did her mother know, Tana would indeed be young almost forever.

"I don't need anyone to take care of me. I'm doing just fine." She could feel her anger rising. "Was that the 'big surprise'?"

"You work at an inn," her mom replied flatly, pointedly not answering her question. "Plus, the Branson boy was coming. And he's always been such a good-looking man."

"I *manage* an Inn. And Paul Branson is an uptight prick who I'm pretty sure cheated on his wife with the nanny, the maid, and the pool boy."

"That was before dear," her mother said, "and they separated."

Tana pushed her parfait away, standing up. "I think we're going to settle in. See you in the morning." She walked out, knowing Amon would follow.

They walked up the stairs down the massive corridor until they finally made it to her room. It was just as she'd left it. The walls were cream and so was most of the furniture. There was no kind of personalization to it, no decoration. And this wasn't because she moved, it was always like this. Now there was a TV for guests, so that was a nice touch.

Amon walked the room, looking around. "Hm. You used to be boring, didn't you?"

She snorted. "By force I suppose." She flopped down to the bed. Say what you will, but the bed was delectably soft.

"You were excellent out there, bunny."

"Hardly," she scoffed.

"Of course you were. You stood up for yourself, even after everything that's happened. You are truly brave." Tana's face was on fire. Amon turned back to his natural form, and she felt even more relaxed. As much as she wished her parents weren't like this, it was nice to have backup afterward. He let Tana deal with it without jumping in and trying to come to her rescue. She didn't need to be rescued, but she loved knowing she had support.

He rounded the bed to join her, pulling her in close from behind. "You know what, I think we should relax and watch a movie. I'm sure they have some sort of streaming service in here."

Amon moved to the TV and started messing around until the screen was on and he'd found a remote. Tana had moved to the bed, ready to relax after everything that had happened. "I just can't believe them. I mean, I know I didn't do what they wanted, but I'm fine. I'm successful and going to school."

"I couldn't agree more," Amon said. He pulled up a list of movies then plopped on her side so they could browse.

"Oh, that one," Tana said.

"Summer of the Toxic Crocodile Man?" Amon questioned.

"I like scary movies. And someone said this one was awful. Those are the best."

"Whatever you say, bunny." Amon put the movie on and they relaxed into each other.

The movie was just as ridiculous as she thought it would be.

At one point, the Crocodile man was chasing a boat through the swamp. It got silent and when he finally broke through the water at the boat, Tana gasped in fear. Amon moaned in delight. "Are you too into Crocodile man?" she asked.

"No," he breathed. "Your fear is heaven."

"What does it taste like?" Tana was so curious—and a bit self-conscious—about her taste.

"Well, most fear is sort of bland or slightly savory. Yours is sweet and full of flavor. I don't think I'll ever get enough."

Tana blushed deeply at that. "Oh."

"Well, there's only one thing that rivals that taste."

"What?"

"Let me show you," he said, making his way down her body.

And, boy, he showed her.

23

AMON

The next morning Amon rolled over and Tana was gone. He groaned and got up, planning to find her.

"Yes, I understand. I-," she cut off, listening to whoever was talking. She was in the bathroom. "Okay. I'll let you know in a few days. Yes, bye." A second later, Tana carefully opened the door and screamed when she saw Amon standing there. Her brief amount of fear flowed through him, sending shivers down his spine. "Jeez. I thought you were asleep."

"I was. Who were you talking to?" he asked.

"Mrs. Camden. She's selling the inn."

"What?"

"Yeah. After the whole getting snowed in thing she realized it's too much stress for a woman her age and wanted to tell me first since..." she trailed off.

"Since what?"

"It's stupid," she dismissed, crossing her arms.

"Tell me anyway."

"I've always wanted to buy it. Even though it stresses me

out, I love my job and have always wanted to own my own inn. I thought if I stayed at the inn and saved everything I could, I would be able to buy it when she was ready. But she wants to sell now and there's no way I have enough and the bank won't give me a loan, I'm sure of it, and it's all going to be gone and..."

"Bunny," Amon interrupted. Tana started crying, and he pulled her close. He rubbed her back, trying to soothe her.

"I'm sorry. I shouldn't be crying. It was just a stupid dream."

"It's not stupid. If you want the inn, you'll have it."

"How?" She pulled away from his shoulder, which was now covered in tears and snot. "I don't have it."

"I do. And even if I don't, there's a ton of old stuff in the sitting room that must cost a fortune. And there has to be someone in that magical town that can fake an identity. I can get a loan. We'll figure it out."

He smoothed his hand over her hair. "I couldn't ask you to do that. You love that stuff and..."

"No bunny. I love you. Stuff is stuff."

"What?"

"I love you. You're headstrong, intelligent, and beautiful. Fated or not, I would be an idiot not to love you."

She teared up all over again. "I love you too. But are you sure you want to stay? You could go anywhere now."

"As long as I'm with you, it doesn't matter." She jumped at him, wrapping herself completely around him. He caught her and brought his lips to hers, deepening the kiss.

After a while, Tana pulled away. "As much as I'd like to repeat last night, I'm sure my mother is about to send the maid in to get us for breakfast. And I'm sure she instructed her not to knock."

He huffed a laugh at that but set her on the counter

anyway. "I'm hungry for something else this morning." He moved down her body and went straight for her clit. If they were limited on time, he was going to be sure to use all of it.

24

EPILOGUE

ONE YEAR LATER

TANA

Tana stood on the porch of The Camden Inn. She had decided to keep the name, even though it wasn't hers. The large porch now had an awning above it, courtesy of some dragon shifters Bea knew. That had been one of the first things she and Amon did when the place officially became theirs.

The day Mrs. Camden called, they quickly excused themselves from her parents after breakfast and booked it back to the inn. Tana called Mrs. Camden and told her they needed a few weeks to get things together, but they wanted it. She agreed and they went to work. They sold a few furniture pieces and jewelry from Amon's hoard and he was able to get a new identity and take out a loan. With that, it was pretty simple. Mrs. Camden was fair and just wanted to take the money and cut ties.

Once it was in their name, they got to work remodeling. They didn't want to change everything. The place had a lot of charm and an antique vibe they wanted to keep. However,

Tana did throw all those floral duvets away as soon as the paperwork was signed.

Now, it was equal parts modern and antique. The floral wallpaper in the lobby was now sage green with a mural of flowers Tana painted. At first, she hadn't had the confidence to paint something so large, but once she had the vision in her head, and all the supplies, she painted it in a few days. Plus, Tana had sewed, crocheted, or painted almost every surface in the place. She made throws for the couches, coasters for the desk and coffee tables, and embroidered hangings for the walls.

Amon started working at a tech firm run by a bunch of vampires. All the reading he'd done while bound taught him a lot and they hired him for their public relations team almost immediately. And lucky for him, all myths aren't true and vampires don't work nights, so he could work a regular nine-to-five. And without the need to save for the potential of buying, it was much easier to move into a spacious apartment in town. They even moved some of Amon's stuff back around the inn with the rest going to their new place downtown. It had been just under a year since they decided to buy the place and she couldn't believe how fast time was going.

Now, it was the holidays again, and because Tana normally dreaded going home, they decided not to go this year. Her mother threw a fit, but Tana hoped she was finally getting the picture.

Tana was sipping her peppermint hot chocolate when she felt a presence behind her. When Amon wrapped his arms around her, she pretended gasped. He loved giving her a good scare, but lately, she'd gotten used to him randomly appearing in places. "I didn't scare you, bunny," he said in her ear.

"How do you know?" she asked.

"I can taste it, remember?"

She hummed and leaned against him.

"Well," he said, "it's a good thing I've been out chopping wood with Tyler." Before Tana could react, he slipped his freezing cold hands under her jacket onto her stomach. This time, she squealed for real. "Now that's what I'm talking about," he said with a grin.

"Whatever. That wasn't fair," Tana pouted.

"All's fair in love and fear, bunny. Isn't that what you humans say?"

She laughed. "Not exactly."

But it was true for them—and she wouldn't have had it any other way.

"You excited for art night tonight?" he asked. Since taking over, they started doing crafting nights at the inn. Guests loved it and people from town even came to join some nights. They did everything from painting to crocheting. Tonight, they were doing pottery and Tana was excited. She waited weeks for those pottery wheels to come in. And to break them in, Amon suggested they invite all their friends for an impromptu art night. She agreed and everyone was coming.

"Yes," she said, "I can't wait. Oh speaking of which, I need to go pick up more clay from the store."

"I thought you went yesterday," Amon said with an eyebrow quirk.

Crap. Tana was hoping to sneak out to the store to get some more yarn for a blanket she was making. Amon supported her fully, but also made sure their house wasn't overtaken by craft items. "I just...want to make sure we have enough," she said with a toothy grin.

"Fine, fine. But just be sure to be back when everyone

gets here." They shared a kiss and she sped off, excited for her new skein of yarn.

The night was going perfectly. Everyone came for dinner first, which Alise was happy to prepare. They shared fun memories about working at the inn and living in town. Not everyone was aware of paranormals, so those parts were left out, but it still made for a great time.

After everyone was done, they moved to the rec room where Bea and Amon set everything up while Tana was out. There were string lights all over and a cute little tree decorated in the corner.

"Wow," Tana said when she got there, "you guys really went all out."

"Yeah, well, we figured it should be festive," Bea said.

Amon stood there silently smiling and blushing at Tana.

"You okay?" Tana asked when Bea walked away to get set up.

"Fine," he replied. She narrowed her eyes suspiciously, but didn't say anything.

"Alright everyone," Tana called. "If you want to take a seat at a wheel, we'll get started. Tana walked to her wheel and sat down. Bea and Amon had set a certain amount of clay on everyone's station to prepare.

When she went to pick up the clay, she noticed something sticking out of the top. It was a ring. The ring had a gold band that branched into a leaf pattern. The leaves were holding a circular ruby in the middle. It was really pretty.

"Hey, Bea I think you dropped your ring in my—"

The words died in Tana's mouth when she turned and

saw Amon on one knee. She looked around and all her friends were gathered, looking at them.

"Tana," Amon started, "this past year has been a whirlwind of new for me. When we met, it felt like everything in my life clicked, and from that moment on, you have been my past, present, and future. You have opened my life up to things I never thought possible, and I could never thank you enough for that. So Tana Kane, will you marry me?"

Tana felt the tears pouring down her face. "Yes. A million times yes!"

He stood and she jumped into his arms, straight into a kiss. She could hear everyone cheering behind her, but she wasn't ready to let go.

"But, we're already mated," Tana whispered to him.

"Yes. But humans get married. And I want us to do it all."

Tana's heart swelled. She released him and he put the ring on her. She gave him one more kiss before going back to her friends who were all gushing just as much as she was. Alise was even crying.

Tana couldn't feel more loved and appreciated than she did in that moment, and she hoped to feel this way forever.

And somehow, she knew she would.

The End

WANT TO READ A BONUS SHORT FEATURING AMON AND TANA?

Read Christmas in Noel NOW!

AFTERWORD

Thank you so much for reading Snowed Inn (With a Demon). This idea originally came to me when I began thinking about writing a novella. And as a holiday lover, I knew I wanted to do something for one of my favorites!

Originally, this was supposed to be a slightly scary book about the Inn keeper and an alpha hole demon falling in love. However, Amon decided very early he was a socially awkward, fluffy boi who just wanted to find love. Plus, Tana wouldn't even look in the direction of anyone who wasn't equally as loving as she was. The ending fluffy product was exactly what it should be and I hope you all agree.

ACKNOWLEDGMENTS

I first want to thank my mom and dad for emotionally and financially supporting my reading habits and encouraging me to follow my dreams. Next, I want to thank my partner Adi, for being so supportive though my writing process and in everything else. And for listening to my ramblings about tail play, even if he had no idea what I was talking about.

I next want to thank all of my indie author friends who supported me through this process. You gave me ideas, feedback, and helped me never give up. You guys have been so great and I can't thank you enough.

Lastly, I'd like to thank you, my reader. This has been my dream for a very long time and you all are making it possible, so thank you.

ABOUT THE AUTHOR

Lexie is a paranormal romance author and avid reader from Upstate New York. She runs an editing and PA company Morally Gray Author Services and lives with her partner, dog and cat. When she's not reading (which is rarely) you can find Lexie playing video games or looking for amazing indie bookstores and vintage shops. Lexie writes cozy books full of smut with simp-y monsters looking for love.

ALSO BY L.E. ELDRIDGE

Washed Up (With a Kraken)

The Witch's Grave

Made in the USA
Middletown, DE
08 February 2025

70599402R00077